Broken Bow

Irene B. Brand

Heartsong Presents

In memory of my husband's grandparents who homesteaded land in Custer County, Nebraska: Jasper H. Brand and Mary A. Miller Hughes Brand, 1884, and Perry M. Dady and Ellen J. Beard Dady, 1882.

A note from the Author:
I love to hear from my readers! You may correspond with me by writing:

Irene B. Brand
Author Relations
PO Box 721
Uhrichsville, OH 44683

ISBN 978-1-59789-456-2

BROKEN BOW

All scripture quotations are taken from the King James Version of the Bible.

All of the characters and events in this book are fictitious. Any resemblance to actual persons, living or dead, or to actual events is purely coincidental.

Our mission is to publish and distribute inspirational products offering exceptional value and biblical encouragement to the masses.

PRINTED IN THE U.S.A.

one

Paula Thompson had run out of options.

She dropped her valise on the floor of the Grand Island, Nebraska, railway station and settled dejectedly on a wooden bench. According to the Waltham watch hanging from the silver chain around her neck, she had a half hour to wait before the train left for Broken Bow. She had spent a miserable week with Aunt Lucy, and it was a relief when her aunt didn't come to the station to see her off.

Paula's mind momentarily shifted from her problems when a cowboy entered the waiting room and approached the ticket window. She had lived among cowboys for years, but she'd never seen a more handsome one. His dark brown eyes gleamed from the depths of the finely chiseled features of his smooth-shaven face. His long fingers swept back the long black hair that grazed his collar. He gazed around the small room while he waited his turn at the window. His eyes met Paula's. She looked away in confusion, her face flushing. Not wanting the cowboy to think she was inviting his attention, she turned her back on him.

A sense of despair swept through her heart as she wrestled with her own problems. Paula had hoped that a visit to her mother's sister would settle her uncertain future. But Aunt Lucy was a reclusive maiden lady who preferred living alone rather than having her niece for company. Her hopes were more dismal now than they'd been when she left home a week ago.

The potbellied iron stove in the center of the room, as well as the body heat generated by many travelers, made the waiting room hot and stuffy. Paula unbuttoned her dark blue cape, with its soft-rolling black fur collar, and moved to another bench at a distance from the wood-burning stove but closer to the ticket window. She removed her bonnet and pushed stray tendrils of her brown hair away from her forehead. Did she imagine it, or was the cowboy staring at her? She refused to turn her head to see and focused on her troublesome situation.

If she was forced to leave the ranch, where could she go? For months, she had prayed for a solution to the problem that had destroyed her peace of mind. Considering her questionable spiritual condition, Paula wondered if God even heard her prayers anymore. Certainly, she was no nearer to an answer now than she had been when she'd learned the contents of Gordon Randall's last will and testament.

She peered at the 1890 calendar hanging on the wall opposite her seat. Four weeks until Christmas. Always before, Paula had looked forward to the celebration of Jesus' birth, but not this year when December twenty-fifth might find her without a home.

Turning slightly in her seat, she cast a covert look at the cowboy. He was wearing the latest creations in clothing for Western ranchers. He had on a gray Stetson hat, its leather band studded with silver. Paula had heard these hats were made by a manufacturer in Pennsylvania and were sometimes called ten-gallon hats, but she'd seen only a few of them. He was dressed in denim pants and jacket, with rivets reinforcing the seams. Paula's stepfather had worn similar clothes made by a San Francisco merchant. The cowboy carried a heavy coat. His boots weren't new, but they were made of expensive hand-tooled cowhide.

Paula's pleasure in the cowboy's appearance turned to alarm when he asked for a ticket to Broken Bow. Paula was suspicious of any stranger who visited her hometown. Could this cowboy be the long-awaited Frank Randall?

Feeling nauseated, Paula put on her bonnet, pulled her cape around her, and walked outside for some fresh air, pacing the wooden platform until the ear-splitting blast of a whistle announced the train's imminent departure. Paula hurried into the station. She picked up her valise and engaged a porter to load the carton of Christmas gifts she'd bought for the Lazy R cowboys. She delayed boarding the train until she saw which car the stranger entered. The conductor motioned him into the second car, and Paula followed at a discreet distance.

Pretending to ignore her quarry, she chose a seat directly across the aisle from him. She placed her valise in the empty seat opposite her to discourage any other passenger from sitting there. The porter put the carton on the seat beside her. Paula snuggled into her cape and covered her legs with a blanket. She didn't expect much heat from the coal-burning stove at the other end of the railroad car. The car had only a few boarding passengers, and no one asked to sit opposite Paula.

She stared out the window as the train left Grand Island and headed northwest. Black clouds moved quickly across the sky, and a brisk wind whipped the brown grass and whirled tumbleweeds across the open prairie. A red-tailed hawk perched on a cottonwood branch, likely surveying the frozen sod for an unwary rabbit or quail. A small herd of antelope grazed on the dried stalks of a harvested buckwheat field. Paula didn't look at her neighbor across the aisle until they passed the next town. However, when the train gathered speed after leaving Ravenna, she glanced in the cowboy's direction. He had laid his Stetson aside, and she admired the sheen of his dark hair. Her eyes roamed over his wide shoulders and dropped to his hands, which held a Bible. He slowly turned the pages, as if searching for a particular scripture to read.

This discovery halted Paula's scheming momentarily. None of the cowboys she knew spent any time studying the Word of God. This stranger obviously wasn't a run-of-the-mill cowhand. Considering his Christian inclination, Paula thought it inappropriate to pry into his affairs, but she was desperate. What if the cowboy turned out to be Frank Randall—the unknown man whose pending arrival had given her nightmares for months?

She opened her valise and took out a box of cookies she had made before she left Aunt Lucy's. "Pardon me, sir," she said.

When he looked up, she lifted the cloth that covered the cookies and extended the box toward him. "Would you like some sorghum cookies? The train won't stop for food between here and Broken Bow. I brought these along in case I got hungry."

"Say! That's kind of you," he said, a smile lighting his brown eyes. "My train was late getting into Grand Island, and I didn't have time to eat."

"Take several," Paula said. "I'm Paula Thompson."

Lifting two cookies from the box with his left hand, the stranger extended his right hand toward Paula. "I'm Carson Hartley."

Relief flooded over Paula as she placed her hand in his

and felt the warmth of his large hand through her gloves. How wonderful to find out that this man wasn't Frank Randall, whom she resented so much! Still, he might be a friend of Randall's, so she must learn why he was going to Broken Bow.

"I live on the Lazy R Ranch about fifteen miles from Broken Bow."

Was her imagination working overtime, or did his eyes take on new interest when she mentioned the ranch?

"I'm stopping at Broken Bow for a few days," he said. "Perhaps you can tell me something about the area."

"I'd be happy to." She removed her valise from the seat opposite her and set it on the floor at her feet.

"Would you like to join me?" she asked, guilt flushing her face. By nature, Paula wasn't devious, and she was ashamed of her actions. She could almost hear her stepfather quoting the proverb, "The folly of fools is deceit." She was well aware that one of the Ten Commandments admonished, "Thou shalt not covet." Yet for almost a year, she had been coveting a ranch that belonged to someone else.

But since she'd gone this far, she might as well find out all she could about Carson Hartley. "It's hard to hear over the wheels on the tracks and the rattling coach," she explained, patting the opposite seat with her hand. "Would you like to sit here?"

❧

Carson put the Bible in his satchel and draped his heavy fur-lined coat around his broad shoulders. He sat down facing her, welcoming this opportunity to learn more about his companion. When their glances had crossed in the railway station, he noticed a despondent, almost desperate look in her eyes. Her blue bonnet, trimmed with a velvet bow and wide satin rosettes, complemented the dark shade of her eyes. She had pushed the bonnet to her shoulders after sitting down, allowing him a view of her light brown hair waving back from her forehead into a neat roll at her nape. On closer observation, he decided that Paula was younger than he had thought—probably still in her teens. When she removed her gloves to take a cookie, he noticed that she wasn't wearing rings.

Having passed his twenty-seventh birthday, Carson knew it was time for him to take a wife. Hadn't his parents reminded him of the fact numerous times? Carson believed that God was actively involved in the lives of His followers, and he had placed the matter of finding a suitable mate in God's hands. Could she be sitting across from him right now? He had expected this trip to Broken Bow to make a dramatic change in his life. Would this coincidental meeting with Paula Thompson also affect his future?

Carson stretched his long legs into the aisle and settled down for a talk. "So how long have you lived in Custer County?"

"Fifteen years. I lived in Grand Island until my mother married Gordon Randall and we moved to his Lazy R Ranch." Humor seemed to brighten her eyes for a moment. "People call it 'Treasure Ranch.'"

The idea of a hidden treasure sparked his interest, so he said, "Treasure Ranch? There must be a story behind that name."

The anxiety on Paula's face faded, and the beginning of a smile lifted the corners of her lips.

"It's a myth more than a story, but I'll tell you what I know about it. When Dad settled in Nebraska, he heard the tale of a miner who had struck it rich in Colorado. The

man was on his way back East when he died from cholera.
During his delirium, he rambled on about some gold he'd
buried. Those who heard the miner talking believed the
hidden treasure was on the land Dad settled. He thought
it was a hoax, but he often caught fortune hunters digging
on his property. As far as we know, no one found anything.
We haven't seen anyone searching lately, so that may mean
someone did find the gold. Or it could be that people have
finally decided the story wasn't true."

"It's an interesting story, though. Are your parents still
living?"

Her sunny expression faded into sadness. She shook her
head. "My mother died five years ago, but I continued to
live with Dad, who's the only father I can remember. He
died almost a year ago."

Her stepfather's death was apparently still fresh in Paula's
mind, for her lips trembled.

Disturbed by the bitterness in her voice and the despair
in her eyes, Carson said softly, "I'm sorry."

Tears moistened her eyes, and the worry of the past year
came tumbling out. "I may have to leave my home."

When she hesitated, he said, "Let's talk about something
else. I don't want to distress you."

Her even white teeth nibbled nervously on her lower lip,
and she shook her head. "I've kept my feelings bottled up
too long. I need to talk, but I shouldn't burden a stranger
with my problems."

"I'm used to having people share their concerns with me.
Tell me anything you want to."

❧

Paula's hands clenched in her lap, and her lids slipped
down over her eyes. They traveled several miles without

speaking, the silence broken only by the murmuring of an elderly couple sitting a few seats from them and the occasional snore of a traveling salesman who had gone to sleep near the other end of the car.

Uncertain whether she should tell this stranger about her problems, Paula raised her eyes to find Carson watching her. The compassion gleaming from his dark eyes encouraged her. As the train rumbled northwest, they munched on sorghum cookies, and Paula explained the situation that threatened to disrupt her life.

"After Mother died, Dad indicated a few times that the ranch would be mine when he was gone, but he died suddenly last Christmas Day after a heart attack. I went to his lawyer, Homer Sullivan, only to learn that Dad's will had been made before he met my mother. His entire estate went to his nephew, Frank Randall."

Resentment filled Paula's heart again as she recalled the disappointment she had experienced when the lawyer read the will.

"Eulie Benedict, the ranch foreman, went with me to see the lawyer, and Eulie became quite angry when he heard the contents of the will. He shouted, 'Why, that can't be! I heard Gordon say more'n once that the ranch would go to Paula.' His word wouldn't hold in a court of law, so the lawyer suggested I look for an updated will."

Again, Paula grew silent, staring at the brown landscape, remembering the disappointing search she and her companion, Florence Davis, had made for another will. Despite their efforts, they had found nothing, and she shook her head to dispel that memory. The clatter of the train along the rails seemed louder than usual as she forced a smile.

"But the cloud may have a silver lining," she continued.

"Dad always carried a box of medical supplies when he and the men were out on the range for several weeks. When the men started preparing for the spring roundup, Eulie found an envelope in the box that contained an addendum to Dad's will, giving the ranch to me if his nephew can't be located within a year of Dad's death. If Frank Randall doesn't return by Christmas Day, the ranch will be mine. If he does, I'm out of a home."

Carson took another cookie from the box that Paula held out to him.

"No wonder you've been worried!" he sympathized. "What do you know about the nephew?"

"Not much. He was born at the Lazy R, but he was a baby when his parents moved away. As far as I know, none of them ever came back."

"Then how did you know where to look for him?"

"We found some old letters in Dad's desk written by his sister-in-law. One of them thanked Dad for making her son his heir. The letters were over twenty years old. The lawyer used addresses from those envelopes to send letters to Mr. Randall, notifying him of the inheritance. Two of the letters were returned, but the lawyer hasn't had an answer from the third one. I know it's unchristian for me to hope he doesn't return, but I hate to lose my home."

"The Bible tells us to cast all our fears on God and that He will sustain us. Whether or not you stay at the ranch, you can trust your future to God."

"I'm not so sure about that," Paula said. "I have a feeling that God isn't very sympathetic toward me. I resent Frank Randall, who's never contacted Dad in the fifteen years I've been in the family. I stayed on after my mother died, made a home for him, and helped with the ranch bookkeeping.

His nephew has done nothing, but he may end up with the ranch. I don't think that's fair!" Considering the injustice of the situation, Paula's lips trembled.

"Perhaps the nephew didn't know where to contact his uncle."

"That's possible, of course. To tell the truth, it hurts my conscience that I'm being so selfish. But I'm worried about my future."

Carson didn't answer, and fearing that he might believe she was selfish, Paula stopped talking. The car seemed darker. Paula wiped the fog from the window and looked out. It wouldn't be long until darkness settled over the prairie. After they passed through Litchfield, the conductor entered and lighted two lamps attached to the walls of the car.

"We'll soon be entering Custer County," he said and nodded toward Paula. "I remember you, missy. You went to Grand Island a week or so ago." He eyed Carson. "I don't remember seeing you before. You a stranger?"

"Yes. I'm from Kansas."

The conductor's round face spread into a wide grin, and his eyes sparkled with mirth.

"I ought to call out like some conductors do when strangers come by train to Custer County."

"I'm sure I'd enjoy hearing it," Carson commented.

The conductor threw back his head and bellowed, "You have just crossed the line into Custer County, Nebraska. PREPARE TO MEET YOUR GOD!"

Bent over double, laughing at his own joke, the conductor moved down the aisle to the next passenger car.

Amused at the man's obvious pleasure in telling a time-worn joke, Carson said, "Was it really that bad?"

"The early history of this county was stormy, or so I've

been told," Paula said. "It was great cattle country, and when the farmers moved in, there was plenty of fighting between the ranchers and the homesteaders. Several people were killed."

When they passed the village of Berwyn, Paula said, "Only a few more miles now."

Carson wiped steam from the smoky window. He stared out the window with apparent interest as the train crept slowly past the stockyards into the town of Broken Bow.

"I'm sure everything will turn out all right for you," he said, patting her gloved hand. "Thanks for the cookies. I've enjoyed talking with you."

Paula blushed, and she wouldn't meet his eyes.

"I liked visiting with you, too, but my motives weren't completely honest. I'm ashamed to admit that when you bought a ticket to Broken Bow I thought you might be Dad's nephew. I just had to find out."

His low chuckle encouraged her. "Think nothing of it. In your situation, I might have done the same thing." As the train ground to a halt beside the small station, he added, "I hope to see you again soon."

"You'll be welcome at the Lazy R as long as I'm there." She hesitated before adding, "How long are you staying in Broken Bow?"

"I have some business to take care of, and I'm not sure how long that will take. I'll probably be here several days." He picked up Paula's cartons, as well as his own satchel, and followed her down the steps to the wooden platform. He placed her boxes inside the station. "How far is it to a hotel?"

"It's only a short walk to the Inman Hotel," she said, pointing southward. "Or you can try the Pacific Hotel.

There are several boardinghouses, too. You'll find everything you need around the town square."

"Is there someone meeting you, or are you spending the night in town?"

"The foreman of the Lazy R will be here soon. I'll wait inside until he comes."

Carson removed his hat and took Paula's hand. "I'll see you again before I leave Broken Bow."

She stared after Carson as he walked away, suddenly realizing that their entire conversation had revolved around *her* affairs. He hadn't divulged any information about himself. Paula's suspicions surfaced again. Why had Carson Hartley come to Broken Bow?

≈

Carson hesitated to leave Paula alone, but when the train pulled out and the stationmaster came inside, he stepped outside and started uptown just as a man wheeled a buckboard into place before the station. Darkness prevented him from seeing the horses' brands, so he paused to be sure that this was Paula's escort. A man jumped down, tied the team, and went inside. Soon he returned to the buckboard with Paula's belongings. Satisfied that Paula was in good hands, he pulled his hat low over his forehead as protection from the wind and headed toward the town square.

two

Paula was chatting with the stationmaster when she heard Eulie's anxious voice at her elbow.

"I saw a stranger outside the station. Did he come in on the train?"

She turned toward the Lazy R foreman and answered quietly, "Yes, and I talked with him. His name is Carson Hartley, so I don't have to worry about *him*."

Eulie squeezed her hand. "I've missed you. I've already loaded your things, so as soon as you're ready, we can go."

The north wind carried a hint of snow, and walking beside him, Paula wound her cape more tightly around her body. "How are things at the ranch?"

Taking Paula's arm to help her into the buckboard, Eulie said, "We've been moving the cattle into sheltered areas where we can feed them if there's a blizzard."

Climbing up beside her, Eulie flicked the rumps of the matched sorrels with the tip of his leather whip. "What's Hartley doing in Broken Bow?"

"He didn't say. He's from Kansas, but since none of those letters from Dad's sister-in-law were mailed in Kansas, I'm sure he's all right."

"I'll keep my eye on him anyway."

Annoyed, Paula said, "I told you there's nothing to worry about. If he'd been Dad's nephew, he would have said so. He has nothing to lose."

"No, but we do," Eulie retorted.

Paula resented his attitude. She appreciated the work Eulie did at the ranch, and not knowing what she would do without his help, she hadn't repulsed his increasingly proprietary attitude. Since his interest in her had surfaced after her stepfather's death, her friend Florence had warned Paula that Eulie was after her inheritance. She suspected that Florence was right, and she had ignored all of Eulie's romantic overtures.

Paula could settle her predicament of finding a home if she lost the ranch by getting married. She would be twenty on her next birthday, and most girls her age were already married. There were many eligible bachelors and widowers in Custer County, but none of them appealed to her as a husband. Neither did Eulie, and she had evaded a direct answer to all of his offers of marriage.

Eulie was a barrel-chested man in his early forties. He had a square, stubborn jaw and a jutting chin, which hinted of his overbearing personality. His graying mustache matched his bushy eyebrows. But the foreman was a good hand, and he now gave his full attention to the frisky team until they put Broken Bow behind them. As they traveled southward toward the Lazy R, Paula pulled the cape over her head, for the wind was strong and the air had a bite.

"How did your visit turn out?" Eulie asked when he had the sorrels trotting to his satisfaction.

"Not good," she said. "I can't live with Aunt Lucy—it wouldn't be pleasant for either of us. So I don't know what to do if Dad's nephew shows up."

"You can marry me. I'll take care of you."

Paula was irritated that she had provided that opening. "Where are *you* going to live? If I lose the ranch, you might not have a home either."

"I'll take care of you," he insisted.

"Thanks, but I'm not ready to marry, and you should stop talking about it. We aren't suited for marriage."

Testily, he said, "We'll never know 'til we try."

"And then it would be too late. Just forget it."

Pouting, the foreman stopped talking. Paula wondered if she would have the courage to fire him if she did inherit the ranch. Eulie usually managed the Lazy R's ten ranch hands with tact, but a few times, Paula had seen his temper erupt into a tongue-lashing, and even physical assault, when a cowhand made a mistake. This had seldom happened when her stepfather was alive, but it seemed to be more frequent during the last year. She had been too timid to reprimand Eulie because she figured she would come off second best in a battle of words with him. But she could control her personal affairs, and she wouldn't marry a man who wouldn't curb his temper.

Paula was chilled by the time they reached the two-story house that her stepfather had built a few years after he settled on the plains. When homesteaders swarmed into the area and filed claims on land already occupied by ranchers, instead of fighting the settlers as many ranchers did, her dad had lived peacefully with them. And when they learned that the land was better suited for grazing than raising crops, the farmers willingly sold their claims to him and moved on.

Lazy R cattle grazed over a few thousand acres now, and the ranch was one of the finest in the state. If the ranch became hers in a few weeks, she could be independent and it wouldn't be necessary to marry to secure her future. But as a single woman, would she be able to operate it as her stepfather had done? As owner of the Lazy R, she wouldn't lack for suitors, but Paula had dreamed of marrying for love. She wouldn't take a husband to acquire a ranch manager.

Unwillingly, she thought of Carson Hartley. He dressed like a cowboy. Judging from the self-confidence and leadership he exhibited, she sensed that Carson was in the habit of giving orders, not receiving them. And he carried himself like a man who had mastery over his emotions. Paula closed her mind to the thought that he possessed all the characteristics needed to take over management of the Lazy R.

Florence opened the door to greet Paula when Eulie stopped the buckboard in front of the house. He carried her satchel and cartons to the porch.

"I'll come up later on to talk about what's happened this week," he said.

Paula's mouth curved into a grimace when Florence snorted. Life would be more pleasant for her if Florence and Eulie got along.

"Has there been any trouble?"

"No," Eulie admitted.

"Then it won't be necessary to do any talking. I haven't had a good week, and I'm going to bed early. Thanks for coming to meet my train."

As she closed the door in Eulie's face, Florence said, "It's been peaceful on the ranch all week. If there was anything to tell, he could have done that on the way home. He just wanted an invite to supper."

Paula took off her cape and boots and gave Florence a hug. It had been fortunate for her that Gordon had hired lank, graying, widowed Florence Davis to live at the Lazy R as Paula's companion when her mother died.

"So you and Aunt Lucy didn't get along?"

"I haven't had a good night's sleep since I left home. Two of her cats usually slept on the bed I was given. If I closed the door and wouldn't let them in, they scratched on the door and meowed all night. If I opened the door, they jumped on the bed. I've had a miserable week."

"I've got a big pan of chicken pie in the oven. You sit here before the fire, and I'll bring your plate to you."

Topped by a mantle carved from a cedar log, a stone fireplace dominated one wall of the living room. Paula held her chilled hands close to the welcome blaze and looked fondly around the room. She had been happy living here with her mother and stepfather. Her stepfather had first lived in a sod house, but later on he had hauled lumber from Kearney, the nearest railroad center, to build the house. A frame home was rare on the plains in the early years because of the scarcity of timber.

Gordon had used one corner of the room for his office, and Paula hadn't changed anything after his death. Leather chairs and a couch were grouped around the large fireplace. Two rockers, where Paula and Florence often sat with their knitting and sewing, were situated close to a big window that provided a view of the rangeland to the north. Paula sat with her feet outstretched to the fire, thinking how good it was to be home. But how much longer would it be her home?

Florence hustled into the room with a tray that held a plate of chicken pie full of plump dumplings, a bowl of applesauce, and a large slice of gingerbread. She had apparently eaten her supper because she only brought in a cup of coffee for herself. Florence sat in the chair beside Paula and sipped on her hot beverage.

When Paula finished her meal, Florence carried the

tray and dishes to the kitchen. When she returned to the warmth of the living room, she said, "Now about Aunt Lucy?"

"We didn't have any trouble, but life with her would be like living in a dungeon. The curtains are closed all the time to keep out the cold in winter and the heat in summer. Even at noon, it's dark in the house. I didn't mention moving in with her, for she's satisfied the way she is, and it wouldn't be fair to force my company on her."

"I wish you'd come with me." Florence's widowed daughter operated a restaurant in Broken Bow, and she wanted her mother to help with the housework and the children. Florence refused to leave Paula, but if Frank Randall returned, Florence intended to live with her daughter. Paula appreciated the invitation, but the daughter's house was already crowded.

She shook her head. "If the nephew does come home, he surely won't be mean enough to put me out without a few days' notice. That'll give me time to make some plans. I'll probably move to a boardinghouse in town and find a job of some kind. I've got enough money to manage for a short time."

Paula wasn't as distressed about moving as she had been. She'd been encouraged by Carson's comforting words that God would take care of her.

three

Carson had finally decided to stay at the Inman Hotel. When he arrived there, the clerk directed him to a second-floor room furnished with a bed, a matching oak washstand with the necessary toiletries, and a small chair. A Lotus square iron heater mounted on a polished-steel base warmed the room. A box of wood was placed behind the stove.

Carson hung his coat on a wall rack. Turning his hat over and over in his hands, he sat in the chair and stared out the steamy window. He had a serious decision to make, and he must make it quickly. Carson clutched his Bible, bowed his head over it, and after a few moments, knelt beside the chair.

"God, I need guidance. I opposed my father to come here, and now I don't know which way to turn. I come to You with the words of Solomon, 'Give therefore thy servant an understanding heart. . .that I may discern between good and bad.' I was already uncertain about what I should do, and meeting Paula Thompson hasn't helped."

It was Carson's habit to present his petition to God and wait for an answer. Sometimes the answer came quickly; at other times he had to wait a long time for direction. When he stood a half hour later, he didn't know what his final decision should be, but God had seemed to say that he should stay in town for a few days.

Carson learned from the hotel clerk that Broken

Bow's population was about one thousand, and in the waning light of evening, he took a tour of the town. He was impressed with the town's business district. He saw banks, several churches, a drugstore, real estate offices, lumberyards, general merchandise stores, and some specialty establishments, as well as blacksmiths and a wagon maker. There were several restaurants, besides the one in the hotel, and he was surprised to see an opera house in a town that had been established only thirteen years ago. The town must have boomed when the railroad arrived in 1886. He noted the office of Homer M. Sullivan, the lawyer Paula had mentioned.

When he returned to the hotel, he walked into the restaurant. Though Paula's cookies had assuaged his hunger for a while, Carson was a hearty eater, and he needed some solid food. He didn't see any vacant tables.

"Would you mind waiting a short time?" the waiter asked.

Before Carson could answer, a man at a nearby table called, "He can share my table."

Smiling, the waiter led the way to the table. The man stood and reached a hand toward Carson. "My name is Bailey. Glad to have company. Are you a stranger to town?"

"Yes. I arrived on the last train."

Bailey was a man of medium height and slender build. His profile was strong and rigid, and blue eyes framed his handsome face. Carson shook hands with the man and sat down opposite him.

The waiter hovered, waiting for an order.

"Our specialty for tonight is fried steak, potato cakes, and baked cabbage. Also, we have soda biscuits and rhubarb jelly."

"That sounds like a feast to me. I've heard about Custer County's good beef. Go ahead with your meal," Carson said to his tablemate as the waiter headed toward the kitchen. "I'm Carson Hartley. I appreciate sharing your table."

"Glad to have you."

"I've walked around the square, and I've gathered that Broken Bow is an up-and-coming town. Are you one of the town's businessmen?"

Bailey laughed heartily. "Depends on what kind of business you mean. I'm in the business of saving souls—I pastor one of the churches in town."

Carson stared at his companion momentarily. Would he ever doubt God's leadership in his life again? He offered a silent prayer of thanks that God had led him to this man.

Bailey finished his meal and asked for another cup of coffee. He commented on the growth of the town since the coming of the railroad while Carson did justice to the plentiful and delicious food placed before him. When Carson pushed back his plate, Bailey said, "What brings you to Broken Bow, Mr. Hartley?"

"I'm on personal business, but perhaps the Lord has led me to your town for another reason. I'm an evangelist, and since I received the call to preach three years ago, I've traveled to various towns in Kansas and Missouri to conduct revivals. I'm sometimes called the Cowboy Preacher."

Bailey's brow wrinkled. "Just a minute! I've heard of you. Did you hold a revival in Kansas City last year?"

"Yes, in May. God sent a great outpouring of His spirit. Many souls were saved."

Bailey snapped his fingers. "Then I have heard of you. My brother-in-law lives in Kansas, and he wrote to me about the great revival, giving high praise for your expository preaching. It's a pleasure to meet you."

"God may be leading me to conduct revival services in your town, but I never proceed with plans without the support of the local clergy. Would you and your fellow pastors be interested in sponsoring a series of evangelistic meetings?"

The pastor's eyes brightened. "I certainly would be, and I'm sure the other preachers will be willing to work with us. We don't often have an opportunity like this."

"I walked around town this evening, and I noticed that most of the church buildings are small. If this is a community-wide revival, it might be better if we find a vacant building for the meeting."

Bailey nodded his head emphatically. "That shouldn't pose a problem. A member of our congregation is putting up a new building on the square, and I'm sure he'll let us use the first floor for the meeting."

"The way this is coming together indicates to me that God is in it. What would be a convenient date?"

"It'll depend on how much time you have, but I'd suggest the first two weeks of January. Right now, most of the churches are busy planning Christmas activities. It will take some time to pass the word that we're having services. Attendance will be larger if we wait until after the holidays."

"That will work for me. I work on my father's ranch, and I'm not so busy this time of year. I usually spend a month in a community when I conduct an evangelistic meeting. But I do have one concern—what about weather conditions in January?"

"No one can predict the weather in Nebraska," Bailey

said, his blue eyes sparkling, "so we'll just lay our plans and trust that we won't have a blizzard. I'll call a meeting of the local preachers in a few days."

After making a few more plans with the pastor, Carson returned to his room, well pleased with the day's events. He now had a reason to stay in Broken Bow, which would provide an opportunity to see more of Paula and also to complete the mission that had brought him here in the first place.

He put three sticks of wood in the stove and partially closed the damper to keep the fire burning throughout the night. Pulling a chair close to the stove, he picked up his Bible. Opening it to a favorite passage in the sixth chapter of Matthew, he read aloud: " 'Lay not up for yourselves treasures upon earth, where moth and rust doth corrupt, and where thieves break through and steal: but lay up for yourselves treasures in heaven, where neither moth nor rust doth corrupt, and where thieves do not break through nor steal: for where your treasure is, there will your heart be also.' "

Carson's mind turned to Paula's story about the treasure that had supposedly been buried on the Lazy R Ranch. A strange tale and one that probably wasn't true. Similar stories about buried treasures had circulated throughout the West, and some people had spent their lives searching for quick riches. But Carson knew that happiness couldn't be measured in worldly possessions. Although his father was rich, when Carson felt God's call to speak for Him, he realized that his treasure was in heaven. He wasn't impressed by Ira Hartley's wealth, which had caused the first rift between Carson and his father.

He knelt beside the stove for a prayer of thanksgiving

before he got into bed. He settled comfortably on the feather tick and pulled the heavy comforter over him. His last thoughts were of Paula and of his reason for coming to this thriving Nebraska town.

four

Paula had her first knowledge of the upcoming evangelistic meeting when Grace Farmer, the teacher of a school ten miles west of the Lazy R, stopped by the ranch in early afternoon. Grace was serving her first term as a teacher, having passed her qualifying exam the previous summer, but on Friday, school was dismissed at noon. At eighteen, petite, brunette Grace wasn't much older than some of her students, but the vivacious, friendly girl held firm control over the classroom. Opportunities for learning were so limited in rural Nebraska that parents wouldn't permit their children's behavior to interfere with the opportunity to get an education.

When she joined Paula and Florence in the cozy living room, Paula commented on the new ankle-length green calico dress that matched Grace's eyes.

"I made two new dresses for the Christmas festivities," Grace said. "I've got another one to wear to the school's Christmas program and box social next Saturday night. Are you coming?"

"I wouldn't miss it," Paula said. Mischievously, she added, "Getting all dressed up for the social must mean that you want someone special to buy your box."

Grace wrinkled her nose and giggled. "I wish that bashful homesteader living near the schoolhouse would, but he's so shy he blushes if I look at him. Of course, I don't suppose he has a dime of extra money, and since I want to make enough money to buy lots of Christmas treats for my students, I should wish for a rich merchant from Broken Bow to buy it."

"A lot of matchmaking was done at box socials in my day," Florence recalled. "But my rheumatism has been acting up, and I won't venture out in the cold night air."

"We'll miss you, but I'm glad you're coming, Paula. A lot of cowboys try to figure out which box is yours, and since you always decorate your box so fancy, they usually guess which box you brought. That's why the bidding is so high—they want to be your companion for the evening."

"And the interest will be even greater this year since she stands to inherit this ranch," Florence said pointedly as she threaded her knitting needles through the pair of socks she was making.

"You make it sound like that's the only reason a man would want to eat supper with me," Paula said reproachfully.

Looking wise as an owl, Florence retorted, "It's had an effect on some people."

Grace seemed puzzled over their exchange, but when no explanations were forthcoming, she inquired, "I also stopped by to see if you'll go into Broken Bow with me today. Reverend Bailey wants to decorate the church for Christmas, and he's organized an outing tomorrow to get a Christmas tree and some greenery for decorations."

"Not many trees around here to cut," Florence stated.

"I know, but a German farmer who lives north of Merna went to Cedar Canyon and cut down some trees and gathered lots of single branches. Because decorating a Christmas tree originated in his homeland, he likes to provide trees for anyone who wants them."

"The only Christmas tree we had when I was a girl

was a plum branch decorated with a few wads of cotton," Florence said.

Paula stirred from her chair and pulled aside a curtain. A few inches of snow lay on the ground, but the sun was shining.

"Why don't you go, Paula?" Florence insisted. "You've been moping around for days, and you need to get out of the house."

"All right, I'll go. It sounds like fun."

"We can stay at my sister's," Grace said. "Since it might be late before we get back tomorrow, take some extra clothes, and we'll plan to stay overnight. Kitty's husband is elk hunting in the Sand Hills, and I know she'll be glad to have us."

"We might as well attend Sunday preaching before we come home," Paula suggested.

Grace giggled. "You must have heard about the new preacher."

"New preacher! What happened to Pastor Bailey?" Florence asked.

"Nothing. But a preacher has come to town to hold revival services, so Pastor Bailey might ask him to preach Sunday morning. When Kitty sent me a note about the outing, she mentioned the preacher and said he was young and handsome." She giggled again. "I bet he won't have any trouble getting a crowd to attend his meeting."

Paula's heartbeat quickened, and she asked, "What's his name?"

Grace thought for a few minutes. "I can't remember. I'd never heard the name before—Dawson, Lawson— something like that."

"Carson Hartley!"

"That's it!" Grace exclaimed. "Then you have heard about him?"

"I met him on the train when I came back from Grand Island, but I didn't know he was a preacher."

As Paula related her meeting with Carson, she was conscious of Florence's speculative eyes watching her, no doubt wondering why Paula hadn't mentioned the man. Even though he wasn't Frank Randall, Paula hadn't stopped wondering who Carson was and why he'd come to Broken Bow. Now the mystery was settled, and she looked forward to seeing him again.

❦

Paula and Grace arrived in town in late afternoon. They left their horses in a livery stable before going to Kitty's three-room frame house near the railroad tracks. Kitty, who resembled her sister in appearance and disposition, opened the door and threw her arms around Grace.

"Surprise!" Grace said. "I talked Paula into coming with me!"

"Do you have room for me?" Paula asked when Kitty took her hand, drew her into the house, and shut the door.

"I've been so lonesome this last week, I'd take in any vagrant," Kitty joked, as she hugged Paula. "Take your things into the south bedroom. I'll have supper ready shortly."

Paula shivered as she and Grace entered the unheated bedroom.

"I've got a pot of black bean soup on the back of the stove," Kitty called from the kitchen. "I'll stir up the fire to heat the soup and make some biscuits. I would have had supper ready, but I didn't know what time you'd get here."

Paula and Grace didn't loiter in the cold room and soon

joined Kitty in the combination kitchen and living room. They backed up to the iron stove to soak up a little warmth while Kitty placed bowls and plates on the table. The smell of perking coffee whetted Paula's appetite.

"I knew you'd have a cold ride," Kitty said. "When I went to the post office to pick up my mail, I thought the wind would blow me away."

Grace filled her sister in on all the things her students had been doing while the biscuits baked; then Kitty filled the bowls with soup, and they gathered around the table.

"Anything new going on?" Grace asked.

"Just the new preacher who's in town, but I told you about that in my note."

"Paula already knew about him. She met him on the train when she came back from Grand Island a few days ago."

"What's he like?" Kitty asked.

Paula felt her face coloring, and she hoped the dim light in the room would keep the others from noticing. "He's young—probably in his twenties. We talked quite a bit. He's from Kansas City, but he works on a ranch."

"I've heard he's called the Cowboy Preacher," Kitty said. "I saw someone I didn't know going into the hotel today; I thought he might be the preacher, but the man I saw doesn't fit your description."

Paula laid down the spoon she held and clenched her hands as a wave of apprehension swept through her.

"You didn't hear this man's name?" Paula asked, trying to speak calmly. She knew she hadn't disguised her concern when Kitty and Grace looked at her sympathetically.

"No," Kitty said. "I'm sorry I mentioned it. A lot of people stop over in Broken Bow on their way to other parts of the country."

"I know, and I'm sorry to be so foolish. But I just feel unsettled—not knowing what might happen. If Frank Randall comes, I'll get on with my life somehow. It's the uncertainty that worries me."

"I'd feel the same way," Grace said, "but I'm sure everything will work out all right."

"I try to convince myself of that," Paula said. "I know I shouldn't wish away time, but I'll be glad when Christmas gets here."

"Try not to worry about it tonight," Kitty said. "You want to be fresh for tomorrow's outing."

Paula always knelt beside the bed for her nightly prayers, but at home, her bedroom was heated from the downstairs fireplace through a metal floor grill. Tonight, she quickly donned her flannel nightgown and crawled into bed beside Grace to say her prayers. While she prayed, a verse came to mind, calming her spirit, and she concluded her prayer time by whispering, " 'The Lord is my helper, and I will not fear what man shall do unto me.' "

Paula repeated the words over and over until she went to sleep.

five

Kitty roused her guests before daylight the next morning. "Time to get up! Come and get your breakfast. We don't want to be left behind."

Still sleepy, Paula slipped out of her nightgown and washed quickly in the hot water Kitty had provided. Grace stretched like a lazy cat and threw the heavy comforter aside. She was dressed by the time Paula finished.

Kitty had a hearty meal ready for them. "This is going to be a long, cold day," she said. "It snowed another inch or two last night, so we can travel in sleds as Reverend Bailey wanted us to do. He thought it would be more festive to go on sleds, which reminds him of the sleigh rides that his parents used to enjoy in the East."

She placed a bowl of cooked dried peaches, a rice pudding, fried bacon, and a pot of coffee on the table. She took a plate of cold biscuits, left over from the night before, from the corner cupboard.

"What time will we get back?" Paula asked as she filled her plate. In spite of the worry of the past year, she had kept a good appetite.

"Late afternoon, I'd judge. It's several miles to the farm, and we're going to eat our noon meal there. I made a batch of apple tartlets yesterday, and some of the other women are taking food, too."

Obviously, even the prospect of a long sled ride in the cold weather couldn't dampen Grace's good spirits, and a wide smile brightened her face. "It's going to be a nice day," she said.

"Should we get our horses from the livery stable?" Paula asked as they left the house an hour later.

"No," Kitty said. "Reverend Bailey has arranged for enough sleds to haul all of us and the greenery. It will be warmer if all of us crowd together instead of riding horseback. After we return, we'll decorate the church. I hope you're going to stay another night."

"Yes, we're planning to stay," Grace said.

When they walked past a hotel fronting on the square, Kitty nudged Paula.

"See the man standing on the hotel steps? That's the other one I told you about."

Paula looked at the stocky, middle-aged man with sandy-colored whiskers. He had a woolen hat pulled low over his eyes and ears. But she refused to allow his arrival to put a damper on the day's pleasure.

Paula was disappointed that Carson was nowhere in sight when they arrived at the square. He hadn't been out of her mind since she'd met him, and she had hoped he would join the outing today. Now that she'd learned he was a preacher as well as a cowboy, she didn't know what to say to him. When he soon came down the street driving Reverend Bailey's team of bay mares that pulled a wooden sled, sleigh bells jingling on the horses' harness, the strange surge of pleasure she felt amazed her. Carson handled the reins expertly as he drew the team to a halt. It was obvious this wasn't the first time he'd driven a team of horses.

Paula didn't want to seem forward in greeting Carson, so she tried to stay hidden among the group of people, young and old, who had gathered for the outing. As his eyes roved over the crowd, she wondered if he was looking for her, but she squashed the idea. During the week he'd been in Custer County, he'd probably met many girls, and for all she knew, he might have a wife in Kansas.

Three more sleds arrived, one of them driven by Reverend Bailey, who stood up on his sled and called out, "Load up! We've got a big day before us."

"There must be thirty people going!" Grace said excitedly as the small crowd surged toward the sleds. "There won't be any room for the trees."

"All of us will crowd on three sleds coming back, and one sled will be reserved for the greenery," Kitty said.

Several of the unmarried girls made a beeline for Carson's sled, so Paula turned toward a sled driven by one of the older townsmen. A strong hand on her arm stopped her.

"Come, Miss Thompson, there's room for you on my sled. You and Reverend Bailey are the only people I know. It would be kind of you to keep me company today."

Paula glanced up at him shyly, thrilled by the pressure of his hand. "I'm glad to meet you again, *Reverend* Hartley. You didn't mention that you were a preacher," she said.

As she walked beside him to the sled, Paula sensed envious looks from several of the other girls. Carson made room for her on the seat beside him and covered their laps with a heavy blanket. A half-dozen other men and girls were already seated on the sled.

Under cover of the jubilation of the crowd, Carson said quietly, "There didn't seem to be any reason to mention my calling when I met you. Besides, I don't like to be called Reverend. I'm only a cowboy the Lord called to preach. Have you heard that I'll be holding revival services during the month of January?"

"Yes, my friend Grace told me."

Reverend Bailey cracked a whip over the head of his team, and they lunged forward in their collars. The other teamsters followed. Carson's team was third in line.

Shouts of laughter and singing echoed around them as the revelers sped out of town. The sled runners coasted easily over the snow, and a brisk wind whirled snowflakes through the air. Paula snuggled deeper into her gray wool coat with its triple cape. She pulled the wool scarf Florence had knitted closer around her face.

"It's a perfect day for a Christmas excursion. I'm glad Florence and Grace talked me into coming along. I've been sort of moody this week."

Carson glanced at her. "No more problems, I hope," he said quietly, and she believed he was genuinely concerned about her future.

"No, but the cold, snowy weather has kept me close to the house. With the deadline almost here, I can't stop thinking about it."

"I'm sure everything will turn out for the best," he said, and Paula was comforted by his words. In spite of the frigid wind that stung her face as the horses broke into a slow gallop, she decided to enjoy herself.

Reverend Bailey started singing, and the words of a Christmas carol wafted to them on the wind. Carson's deep voice took up the refrain, and the others joined in:

> "Hark! The herald angels sing,
>   'Glory to the newborn King;
> Peace on earth, and mercy mild,
>   God and sinners reconciled!' "

They reached their destination before noon, and several of the women volunteered for cooking duty. The farmer had provided a stack of wood, and Paula and Kitty carried armloads to fuel the fire that the men started.

"Be sure to make lots of coffee," Reverend Bailey said. "Carson and I will choose a couple of trees. The rest of you pick out some branches that can be used for garlands."

Although Reverend Bailey threw up his hands in dismay when he saw how much greenery his congregation had chosen, the men soon had two trees and the evergreen branches tied on the sleds, still leaving enough room for passengers. The tangy, spicy scent of cedar was reminiscent of other Christmases, and Paula blinked back tears when she remembered her stepfather's death last year. What had started out as a day of celebration had turned to mourning when she found him dead on the floor of the living room.

Her thoughts shifted to the present when Reverend Bailey announced it was time to eat. Three dutch ovens held baking powder biscuits, two large coffee pots bubbled, and Paula inhaled the tantalizing aroma of a pot of beef stew. With full plates and cups, the men hunkered down near the fire, and the women sat on the sleds while they ate. The sun had chased away the snow flurries, and puffs of white clouds moved swiftly across the sky.

One of the women had brought a custard base, which she mixed with some clean snow to make ice cream.

"Wow! This is good," Grace said, her teeth chattering as she spoke, "but I'm freezing now."

When they started home, Paula joined Grace on the sled driven by Reverend Bailey. Carson slanted a questioning look in her direction, but he didn't ask her to join him. They returned to Broken Bow by late afternoon where darkness was already settling over the town.

"Let's meet at the church at seven o'clock!" Reverend Bailey shouted above the uproar of the revelers. "That will give you a couple of hours to thaw out and eat your supper. Bring some popped corn for garlands."

"Cline's Store was expecting crates of cranberries on the morning train," Kitty said. "I'll see if I can buy a few pounds. They'll look pretty with the popcorn."

"And bring scraps of colorful calico for tree decorations," the pastor added.

&

The interior of the church was plain and somber with its gray painted walls and narrow windows. But two hours after the crowd gathered to decorate, the sanctuary had taken on a festive air. Garlands of cedar, intertwined with strings of popcorn and cranberries, were draped over the windows. One tree, set in a bucket of wet sand, was covered with scraps of red calico and had twenty candles tied to its branches to be lit during the Christmas Eve service. The other tree had been set up outside and decorated with sheaves of wheat and ears of corn to provide a feasting place for the birds.

While they worked, Carson didn't approach Paula, and she fretted all evening. Had she offended him? But when their work was complete and Pastor Bailey asked them to join hands for a closing prayer and song, Carson was immediately by her side. He gripped her hand tightly as the pastor prayed, and they all joined in singing "Away in a Manger." They closed the hymn with the words, "And fit us for heaven to live with Thee there," and Paula sang it as a petition to God.

Carson tugged gently on Paula's hand and pulled her

toward the door. When they stood beside the decorated tree on the lawn, he whispered, "Did I do something to offend you?"

"Why, of course not! What gave you that idea?"

"You didn't ride back with me."

"I rode with my friend Grace and her sister, Kitty. We're staying at Kitty's home. Grace was the one who asked me to go today, and I didn't think I should desert her," Paula dissimulated, although that wasn't the only reason she hadn't returned to town on his sled. She was becoming too interested in Carson, and when he left Broken Bow, she didn't want her heart to go with him.

"May I walk with you to your friend's home?" Carson's soft query interrupted her thoughts.

Paula hesitated. Carson should know that walking a girl home from church was often considered a declaration of keeping steady company. She was attracted to him, but he was only a transient evangelist. Would she provide company for him while he was here, and when he moved to another community, would he forget about her?

Deciding that he probably wanted nothing from her except friendship, she said, "Yes, but let's wait until Grace and Kitty are ready."

"I bought a lantern today, so I'll light it while we wait."

When Grace and Kitty came from the church, Carson cupped his right hand under Paula's arm and held the lantern in his left. They walked closely behind the two sisters, all of them chatting about the day's events. When they reached the house, Grace and Kitty went inside, and Paula paused momentarily on the step.

A freight train rattled by, the shrill whistle piercing the calm of the night, and they couldn't talk for a few minutes.

With the hum of the cars on the tracks receding into the distance, Carson said, "I hope to see you again soon."

"Grace and I are staying for morning worship."

His eyes shone bright in the pale light from Kitty's kitchen window. "Then I'll invite you and your friends to join me for dinner at the hotel after the service. The proprietor sets a good table."

"Thank you. I don't know what time Grace needs to leave town. We'll let you know in the morning."

"I'm going to start visiting ranches and homesteads next week, inviting people to the revival. May I call on you at the Lazy R?"

"Florence and I will be glad to have you."

"Reverend Bailey and I are going to visit north of Broken Bow the first part of next week, but I'll plan to come to your home on Thursday."

"Grace teaches at the local school, and she's sponsoring a Christmas program and a box supper benefit on Saturday night. If you can arrange it, I'm sure she'd like for you to attend."

He squeezed her hand in parting. "I'll make it a point to be there."

Now why on earth did I do that? Paula fretted as she went into the house. Carson's presence at the Lazy R would not only make Eulie mad, but Florence would start speculating.

Grace kidded Paula about her new beau when she went inside, but because all of them were tired and cold after the long day, they soon went to bed. As Paula settled into the feather mattress, she realized this was the first day for almost a year that the possibility of Frank Randall's appearance hadn't been constantly in her thoughts. She'd been so preoccupied with Carson that the threat of the man's possible arrival hadn't disturbed her at all.

Although she was tired, Paula lay awake long after the occasional whistle of Grace's breath from half-closed lips indicated that she was sleeping. Something lurked in the back of Paula's mind that made her feel edgy, and she suddenly realized what it was. Who was the man Kitty had pointed out to her at the hotel this morning?

She supposed she was being foolish, for strangers weren't uncommon in Broken Bow. Men and women often stopped for a few days to rest from a long trip before they continued the final leg of their journey into the Sand Hills or the Dakotas. Her recent vow to quit worrying about losing the ranch surfaced again. Although she was disgusted with herself, Paula knew she wouldn't rest until she found out why the man was in town.

six

Paula dressed for Sunday worship in a brown suit with a three-quarter-length jacket, wide lapels, and enormous sleeves. Her plain skirt was a few inches off the ground, short enough to show her black patent leather shoes tied with grosgrain ribbons. She wore a high-necked blouse. She hadn't brought a hat, so she wrapped a woolen scarf around her head.

Kitty and Grace always liked to sit on the back seat, so they went early before that pew was filled. Paula didn't see Carson when they arrived in the church. When he did enter the door, he removed his soft felt hat and his eyes scanned the sanctuary. Paula sneaked a sideways glance. She wondered if he was looking for her. Reverend Bailey motioned to Carson, and he went forward to sit on the front pew.

He had changed his cowboy clothes for a navy blue worsted suit with a three-button cutaway coat, matching pants, and a white shirt with a high, stiff collar.

When Reverend Bailey entered the pulpit, he remarked, "I asked our guest, Carson Hartley, to bring the morning message, but when he found out that I had prepared a series of sermons with an Advent theme, he declined. We will look forward to having our Kansan brother speak to us in the near future."

Every pew in the sanctuary was occupied, and Paula wondered if that was because the membership thought

Carson would be speaking and they were curious about him. Although Reverend Bailey's messages were always meaningful, Paula, too, had been looking forward to hearing Carson preach.

Reverend Bailey announced the theme of his sermon, "Thank God for who you are," seemingly tying last month's theme of being thankful to this month's Advent messages. He read all of Psalm 139 but chose verse fourteen for his text. " 'I will praise thee; for I am fearfully and wonderfully made: marvellous are thy works; and that my soul knoweth right well.' " His message focused on Mary. Although she had been a humble maiden, she'd been chosen for the important position as the mother of Jesus.

As he talked, Paula looked inward. She had a tendency to doubt her self-worth and compare her qualities with others. She had often wished that she had red hair. She had envied Grace's vivacious personality more than once. In fact, at times, she compared her meek ways to Florence's forthright manner and wished she were more authoritative. Considering that God had created her as she was, when she was critical of herself was she finding fault with God? After all, the Bible said that mankind was made in the image of God.

Reverend Bailey asked Carson to pronounce the benediction, and he quoted from the book of Jude: " 'Now unto him that is able to keep you from falling, and to present you faultless before the presence of his glory with exceeding joy, to the only wise God our Saviour, be glory and majesty, dominion and power, both now and ever. Amen.' "

Reverend Bailey invited Carson to stand beside him to greet the departing congregation. When he shook hands with Paula, Carson said quietly, "You and your friends go to the hotel and wait for me in the lobby, please."

Paula agreed by nodding, but she was flustered by his attention. Had he noticed the blush that she felt rising from her neck to her forehead? When they reached the hotel, Paula asked Kitty and Grace to excuse her for a minute. She walked into the little cubbyhole of an office where the clerk, Isaac Shaw, Florence's brother, was reading the paper.

Isaac looked up at her and smiled.

"Maybe I shouldn't ask, but Kitty told me that another man besides Carson Hartley has come to town. Is he staying here? Do you know who he is and where he's from?"

Isaac flipped through a ledger on the desk and squinted at the entries. "His name is Roscoe McCoy. He listed his address as Albany, New York."

"At least he isn't Frank Randall. I'm tired of wondering if I'm going to lose the ranch. I wish Christmas would hurry and get here."

"All in good time, it will," Isaac assured her.

"Thanks. Florence and I will be coming to town before long to buy a few things before Christmas Day." When Paula rejoined Kitty and Grace, Kitty said, "Your friend must have plenty of money. Food at this hotel is expensive."

"I hope he doesn't keep us waiting very long," Grace said. "I'm hungry."

The words were hardly out of her mouth before Carson entered the lobby with long, purposeful strides. "I have a table reserved," he said. "I took the liberty of ordering for us because I didn't want to delay your return to the ranch."

He held their chairs and seated all of them, and Paula felt like a queen. He hadn't learned such courtly manners on a ranch, and she wondered again about Carson's family background.

Two waitresses placed several trays of food on a nearby folding table, and Carson asked, "Kitty, will you serve the food for us?"

Kitty dimpled prettily and agreed. He had ordered tomato soup, boiled ham, rice croquettes, baked eggplant, pickled purple cabbage, and buttermilk bread, fresh from the oven. Baked apple dumplings covered with thick cream was the dessert of the day.

After their plates were filled, Carson said, "Tell me about Custer County. I've learned quite a lot since I arrived, but I'm sure there are many other things I'd find interesting. You can start by telling me how the town got its unusual name."

"I teach that to my students," Grace said. "In 1880, Wilson Hewitt, a homesteader not far from here, petitioned the government for a post office at his place. He sent in several names for the new post office, but they were rejected. One day when Mr. Hewitt was hunting, he found a broken bow and arrow, and that gave him an idea. He submitted Broken Bow for the town's name, and it was accepted."

"That's very interesting. Paula said that her father came to this area before it became a state, when there weren't any settlements," Carson commented.

"But it filled up pretty fast after statehood in 1867," Kitty said. "Our parents settled in southeast Nebraska first, but they came to Custer County soon after Broken Bow became the county seat. Most of the first buildings were made of sod—even the county offices were located in sod buildings then, although there were a few log houses."

"I'm impressed with the progress made in a few short years," Carson said. "I've seen only a few sod houses, but there are many brick buildings, as well as large and small frame structures."

"Our parents took up a homestead about twenty miles from here, and they've finally gotten a good farm established," Grace said, "even if the January blizzard of '88 did almost wipe them out."

"The snow was bad enough here in town, but it seemed more dangerous out in the country," Kitty added.

"Dad lost a lot of cattle that winter, too," Paula said. "The blizzard lasted for two days, and by the time it stopped, the canyons and hollows were packed with snow. Traveling was out of the question for several days. The cowhands couldn't reach the haystacks, the heavy snow broke down the fences, and the cattle strayed from ranch to ranch."

"Mail wasn't delivered into Broken Bow for over a week," Kitty said. "We survived by killing animals and prairie chickens that swarmed around the farm buildings and by eating the vegetables we had stored in a cellar under the house."

"Let's hope we don't have another blizzard like that this winter, or the proposed revival may have to be postponed." Carson glanced around the table. "Would you like anything else to eat?"

"I couldn't eat another bite," Kitty said.

"Thanks for the dinner," Paula said, "but we should be starting home before Florence sends out a search party. We'll look for you to stop by the Lazy R when you're out that way."

She detected a hopeful, almost eager look in his eyes as he added, "It's been a pleasure to visit with you and your friends. I'll be looking forward to seeing you again in a few days."

As Carson walked with them to the livery stable to get their horses, Paula had never been so blissfully happy, and for the moment, there were no shadows across her heart.

seven

On Thursday, as Carson traveled toward the Lazy R, he looked forward to the coming days with Paula to assess his strong attraction to her. He'd never spent much time thinking about women, but he kept wondering if Paula was the one for him. He wanted a wife and family, and if he married her, it would solve her problem of not having a home if the Lazy R passed to Frank Randall. But he knew it wasn't practical to think that he could court Paula and find out if he really loved her—and just as importantly, if she loved him—before the Christmas Day deadline that would settle the ownership of the Lazy R.

Carson was a cautious man, and he didn't normally make decisions quickly. God had dealt with him for two years before he finally accepted the call to preach the gospel. Taking a wife was a serious decision, and Carson wanted to be sure.

With such somber thoughts on his mind, he rode slowly, taking an appraising look at the Lazy R, pleased that a short warming spell had melted most of the snow. The beauty of the rolling land was impressive. Lakes and small streams were frozen, but flocks of ducks floated on open pools in the small creek that he followed. He didn't see any cattle until he neared the ranch buildings, where large herds were enclosed in fenced areas that would prevent drifting in a blizzard and where they'd be easy to feed. Sturdy Red Polls and Herefords munched the cured hay scattered over the snow.

Carson was happiest when he was working on his father's ranch, and their first serious disagreement had occurred when Ira threatened to sell the property. Selling the ranch was his father's strategy to make his son take over management of the mercantile business. He smiled grimly when he remembered his threat: "If you sell the ranch, I'll leave Kansas and buy one of my own."

Carson didn't have enough money to pay for a ranch outright, but his bank account held enough that he could secure a loan. Ira hadn't sold the ranch, but Carson knew his father hadn't yet given up his dream of having him eventually settle down in the city and become a businessman.

But as he paused on a knoll and looked down at the neat Lazy R buildings protected from the wind by a grove of evergreen and cottonwood trees, Carson was again convinced that he was meant to be a cattleman along with his calling. The frame house had weathered to a dull white luster, and spots of snow clung to the roof. A dozen outbuildings dotted the landscape a short distance from the ranch house. On a hill behind the barn, a windmill whirred noisily in the brisk wind. To Carson, this was the ideal place to work—not cooped up in his father's mercantile establishment in Kansas City. Thoughtfully, he lifted the reins and guided the horse slowly toward the ranch headquarters.

❧

Paula had been watching for Carson, but she stayed in the house until he tied his horse to the hitching post and approached the porch. Florence was right behind Paula as she opened the door, and Paula knew she was quickly taking Carson's measure.

"You could do a lot worse," she hissed in Paula's ear.

Paula turned indignant eyes on her. "Hush! He'll hear you."

Paula greeted Carson and introduced Florence, whose presence kept Paula from feeling self-conscious in his company.

"Make yourself at home, Reverend Hartley," Florence said. "Supper is almost ready."

"I'm not accustomed to being addressed as Reverend. I'm only a cowboy preacher. Just call me Carson."

Paula invited Carson to sit down. "I'm weary of being in the saddle for a few hours, so I'd just as soon stand for a while," he said.

He walked around the room. Pointing to the mounted elk head above the fireplace, he said, "Your stepfather must have been quite a hunter."

"Not so much in recent years, but he hunted in his youth." She pointed out the mounted deer head with an impressive rack of antlers that hung on the outside wall. "Wild animals were plentiful on the range when he first settled the ranch. There's still good hunting farther north in the Sand Hills."

Florence was determined to make an impression on Carson, Paula decided, when the housekeeper called them to the dining room. She'd prepared enough food that all of the Lazy R hands could have eaten with them, and there would still have been leftovers.

She had roasted two wild ducks that one of the cowboys found on the lake behind the barn. The two ducks were arranged on a large platter and covered with an orange sauce. Florence had also prepared hominy, stewed canned tomatoes, baked cabbage, and slaw.

"Do you like coffee with your meal?" Florence asked after they'd gathered around the table and Carson had prayed a blessing on the food.

"Yes, if you please."

They hadn't yet finished supper when Eulie slouched into the dining room through the kitchen door. As the deadline neared without the arrival of Gordon's nephew, Eulie acted more and more as if he owned the ranch and rarely knocked. His attitude hadn't bothered Paula at first. So had Eulie changed, or was she different?

"Oh, excuse me," he said. "I didn't know you had company."

Florence sniffed and attacked the food on her plate.

Paula knew Eulie was lying, for how could he not have known when one of the cowboys had stabled Carson's horse? She swallowed her resentment and introduced him to Carson.

"Mr. Hartley, meet Eulie Benedict, foreman of the Lazy R. Eulie, Carson Hartley from Kansas City."

"Oh, you're the new preacher who's come to town," Eulie commented in a condescending tone.

Carson stood to shake Eulie's hand.

Paula knew that Florence was furious at the foreman's intrusion, and she nudged the housekeeper's foot under the table, hoping that would keep her from making a scene.

"Go ahead with your supper," Eulie said. "My business can wait. I'll just have a cup of coffee with you."

He strolled into the kitchen, returned with a tin cup of coffee, and sat down without invitation opposite Florence. She asked Carson if he wanted seconds. When he assured her that he had finished, she started clearing dishes from the table, banging them and the silverware together. Paula knew they would have some cracked dishes before Florence worked off her anger.

Trying to make the best of an awkward situation, Paula said, "You're in for a treat, Carson." Eulie gave her a sharp look. She assumed this was due to her use of Carson's given name. Flustered, she quickly continued, "Florence made gooseberry pies for dessert."

"I've never eaten any gooseberry pie," Carson commented.

"Gooseberries grow wild in Nebraska's draws," Paula said. "The cowhands pick the fruit, and Florence cans them for use in winter."

"Gooseberries are sour enough to make a pig squeal," Eulie said, "so I hope you put lots of sugar in the pie, Florence."

Florence placed wedges of the pie on plates and served the others before she ungraciously plunked a piece of pie and a fork before Eulie. She set a pitcher beside Carson's plate.

"That's fresh cream," she said. "Cream takes care of the tartness of the berries."

Carson poured some of the thick cream over his wedge of pie and took his first bite.

"Say, that is a good piece of pie! You've prepared a delicious meal. My mother's cook couldn't have done any better." After he ate several forkfuls of the pie, he turned to the foreman. "This is good rangeland, Eulie. I'm a cowman at heart, and I'd like to know about the ranch operation."

"Then why don't you stay over for a day or two, and I'll show you around. There's an empty bed in the bunkhouse."

"Nonsense!" Florence said. "Gordon's bedroom is empty upstairs. There's no need for him to sleep in the bunkhouse."

"Thank you, Florence. I would appreciate staying a few days if that won't put you out."

"Glad to have you," Eulie said.

He acts as if the ranch is his, Paula noted.

"How many cattle will the ranch support?" Carson asked Eulie.

"I usually run three to four thousand, but I'm down from that now as I shipped a few hundred before winter set in. Randall used to run more than that, but we sold a lot of steers when the railroad came through."

As Eulie praised the ranch for its fertile soil and good water supply, Paula noticed how often it was "I" or "we," even when he spoke of the days before the owner's death. She picked at the luscious gooseberry pie, irritated because he had ruined this evening that she'd anticipated with such pleasure.

When there was a pause in the conversation, Paula said, "Florence, if you and Carson will go into the living room, I'll see what Eulie needs." When Florence started stacking the dishes, she said, "We can take care of those later."

She cast a significant glance at Florence, and the woman nodded. "Come along, Carson. It's warmer in the living room. This room can get a mite cold in the winter, 'cause its only heat is what drifts in from the kitchen and living room."

Paula walked into the kitchen, and Eulie followed her.

Conscious of how much she would need this man if she took control of the ranch, Paula suppressed her anger, saying amicably, "Why did you need to see me tonight?"

Speaking loudly, Eulie asked, "What time do you want to leave for the social Saturday night?"

Paula knew his voice had carried easily to the living

room. *Watch your temper!* she admonished herself.

"You don't need to be concerned about that. I've invited Carson to go with me to the box supper. He's the only escort I'll need."

Lowering his voice, Eulie said, "You'd better be careful about taking up with every stranger that comes along. Don't forget you and me have an understanding. I can cause you plenty of trouble if I've a mind to."

"What do you mean by that remark? We do *not* have an understanding."

"Don't matter—we're in this together. And don't forget it!" Raising his voice, he said, "I'll ride along with you to the social. We'd better leave early."

Giving her a warning glance, he left the kitchen, slamming the door harder than necessary.

Tears stung Paula's eyes, and she knotted her hands trying to gain control of her anger before she joined the others in the living room. Even before Carson came to town, the idea of marriage to Eulie had repulsed her, although she feared it might come to that. The thought was intolerable now. Could she be in love with Carson, or did her interest in him stem from the fact that he was different from other men she'd known? She knew a lot of cowboys and a few preachers, but she'd never met a combination of the two.

When she entered the living room, Florence and Carson were carrying on a lively conversation about early days in Custer County.

"I came to this area with my man in the early sixties," Florence was saying. "He was a cattle driver—bringing cattle from Texas to the railroad in Kansas and Nebraska to ship east. When Texas cattlemen realized that this vast area of grassland was empty except for a few natives and a lot of buffalo, they started ranches here."

"Reverend Bailey says that the range wars were bad when the homesteaders started moving in," Carson said.

"That's true. My husband was killed in a ruckus between cowboys and homesteaders. The homesteaders had the law on their side because most of the ranchers had settled without any legal papers. The newcomers were bound to win in the long run."

"Which made it hard on the ranchers, I suppose."

"Oh, there you are!" Florence said when she noticed Paula. "I'll wash the dishes and clean the kitchen now."

"I'll help, too, if Carson won't mind being left alone for a short time."

"I don't mind at all—I'll enjoy sitting here in front of the fireplace and soaking up some warmth."

"I don't need any help," Florence stated flatly. "I want to get things ready for breakfast, too, so it may take me awhile." She cast a meaningful glance toward Paula, who was half-angry, half-amused at Florence's obvious efforts at matchmaking.

Florence stirred the coals in the fireplace and put another log on the fire before she left. For some time, Paula watched the sparks and increasing flame as the fresh wood ignited. Even with Carson nearby, she couldn't keep thoughts about her mother's death and how her stepfather had always treated her like a daughter from coming to her mind. This always led her to wonder why he hadn't provided for her future.

"Excuse me for meddling in your affairs," Carson said, interrupting her reverie, "but is the foreman giving you any trouble?"

"He does get arrogant at times, but he's worked at the Lazy R for several years, as foreman for the past five years. Naturally, he thought he should take over when Dad died. I had been doing the book work for a couple of years, so I knew that part of ranching. But Dad didn't want his womenfolk working on the ranch, so I didn't know much about the work itself. I had to rely on Eulie. The lawyer who's administering the estate has advised me about the finances, but I've let Eulie run the ranch the way he wants to."

"I'm going to continue meddling and offer you a bit of advice. If you do inherit this ranch, remember *you're* the owner, not Eulie."

"I can't operate it without help," Paula said.

Florence rejoined them at that time, and Carson said nothing more about the ranch.

Before they retired for the night, Paula asked Carson to read from the Bible and have prayer. He went to his saddlebags that he'd placed beside the door, got a Bible, and moved his chair closer to Paula.

"I realize you've got a lot of worries, but I urge you to take all your concerns to God. He cares for you. Once when Jesus was talking to His disciples, He said, 'In the world ye shall have tribulation: but be of good cheer; I have overcome the world.' God never puts more on us than we can handle. I'm going to read a portion of Psalm 32. I hope the words of the psalmist will encourage you."

Carson opened his well-worn Bible, found the passage he wanted, and read in a resonant and expressive voice, " 'I will instruct thee and teach thee in the way which thou shalt go: I will guide thee with mine eye. . . . Many sorrows shall be to the wicked: but he that trusteth in the Lord, mercy shall compass him about. Be glad in the Lord, and rejoice, ye righteous: and shout for joy, all ye that are upright in heart.'"

Carson knelt between Florence and Paula, saying, "Let's form a prayer chain." They joined hands.

"Father in heaven," he prayed reverently, his words uplifting Paula more than anything she had heard for a year, "we praise You tonight for the comforting words of the Bible. We know You care for Your people and that You guide us from Your throne in heaven. I pray especially for Paula—give her peace of mind, comfort of heart, and wisdom to make the right choices. You understand the needs of our bodies and souls, so we ask for the Holy Spirit's guidance in the days ahead. Amen."

Paula's eyes were moist when he finished. She squeezed his hand before she released it, but her throat was too tight for words.

&

Carson said good night to Paula, shouldered his saddlebags, and followed Florence to an upstairs room, warmed by a grated opening in the ceiling of the living room. He stood for several minutes, looking around. What stories would these walls tell if they could talk? What secrets would they reveal about the births or deaths that occurred here?

When Carson settled into the bed in Gordon Randall's room, his thoughts were troubled. He had heard every word of the conversation between Paula and Eulie. What had the foreman meant when he warned Paula that he could cause her trouble? Was she romantically involved with Eulie? It was obvious that if Frank Randall didn't come, Eulie intended to marry Paula and take over the Lazy R Ranch. Carson wondered what he could do to ensure that the Lazy R remained Paula's home. Or should he even become involved? Would it be best for him to contact Reverend Bailey, tell him that he would have to cancel the revival, return to Kansas City, and forget he had ever heard of Paula Thompson or the Lazy R?

Carson had lots of questions but no answers, before he finally slept.

eight

The following day Carson asked Paula to accompany him to several ranches and homesteads to extend invitations to the revival. He was pleased when she accepted.

They took the noon meal with a German homesteader, Reinhart Schultz and his wife, Johanna—the young immigrant couple with whom Grace Farmer boarded so she didn't have to travel so far to teach. The meal consisted of a large dish of sauerkraut and roasted venison, finished off with fresh fried doughnuts.

By midafternoon, Paula turned toward the Lazy R Ranch and said, "Grace mentioned that a couple of new children have come to school lately, and she thinks they're living in a dugout on the ranch. I haven't mentioned it to Eulie, for he'd probably make them leave, but I'd like to investigate if you don't mind going with me. There's an abandoned dugout not far from here, and that may be where they're living."

"I didn't know people still lived in dugouts," Carson said, as they turned their horses eastward.

"Very few families do. This one was built by one of the first homesteaders, but it hasn't been used since Dad bought the preemption rights. Most of the dwelling is dug into the side of a bank, with the front constructed of logs and sod. The last time I rode by the dugout, it looked as if it was falling down. I can't imagine how anyone can live there."

When they topped a small rise and rode down the valley where the dugout was located, smoke drifted upward from a piece of rusty pipe extending through the earthen roof of the dwelling. They halted their horses in front of the dugout, and Carson said, "They've fixed it up some—looks like someone's put in a few new logs."

A blond, blue-eyed man pushed back a cowhide that served as a door for the dugout and hurried toward them. Peering at them, fear evident in his eyes, the squatter said, "Ve vant no trouble. Ve going to Anselmo, but the vife is sick. Beg to stay for a few veeks."

A boy and a girl, bearing the same physical features as the man, peered from behind him.

Paula held up her hand. "I won't cause you any trouble. I'm from the Lazy R. I heard someone was living here, and I wanted to see who it was. Do you need any help?"

"Nah—no help, just vant to stay 'til vife better."

"What's your name?" Carson asked.

"Olaf Hannson. Vife's name is Britta. Ve move on soon."

"Very well, Mr. Hannson, you're welcome to stay." Turning to Carson, Paula said, "Do you have paper and pencil in your pocket?"

When he produced the requested items, she wrote, *Permission granted to Olaf Hannson and his family to stay here temporarily*, and signed her name below the words.

Giving the paper to Hannson, she said, "If any Lazy R cowhands come around, show them this note."

As they turned their horses toward the Lazy R ranch house, Paula said, "Another poor immigrant hoping to start a new life in Nebraska! I don't know how they'll ever make it."

"I wonder if they have anything to eat."

Paula grinned. "That hide covering the door of the dugout came off of a Lazy R cow, and not too long ago. So they do have meat. I don't begrudge them a cow, and Dad didn't either. He was always kind to homesteaders, but Eulie is a different matter. I hope he doesn't learn about the Hannsons."

Carson tenderly glanced sideways at her. "Eulie doesn't own the Lazy R," he reminded her softly.

"Neither do I—yet!"

They were getting close to the ranch headquarters when Paula reined in her horse. Pointing to a slight rise in the land, she said, "What do you make of *that?*"

Carson glanced in the direction she pointed. Several holes had been dug in the side of a clay bank. The digging had occurred since the last snowfall. Remembering what Paula had told him about the legend of a buried treasure on the ranch, amusement flickered in his eyes. "Maybe someone is prospecting for gold."

"Why, it's been years since anyone has been digging on the ranch! Who could be doing this?"

"Let's take a look," he said. Lifting his reins, he led the way as they galloped toward the area. Four different holes about three feet deep had been dug in wildly separated areas.

Paula glanced around in obvious disbelief. "I wonder why Eulie and the cowboys haven't seen who's doing this."

"I'd guess this was done yesterday," Carson said, dismounting and looking more closely at the holes. "There's only one set of tracks—and the man wasn't wearing cowboy boots. Only one horse was here, too."

He vaulted into the saddle. "What do you want to do about it?"

Paula shrugged. "Not much I can do. There's no law against digging holes. There's a prairie dog town in this field, and the land isn't good for anything. If someone wants to have fun digging, this is a good place to do it."

❧

Before she had gone to town with Grace, Paula had wrapped the box she would take to the social in white butcher paper and had sketched red Christmas bells and candles on the covering. She made a different kind of box each time, for no one was supposed to know which box a girl brought, but often the girl gave a hint to the man she wanted to buy her box. Eulie had been pestering Paula for weeks, trying to find out what her box would look like. But she had no intention of telling him. On Saturday morning when Carson went to look around ranch headquarters, she knew that would keep Eulie occupied, so she brought her box to the kitchen.

"I've got lots of good things ready for you," Florence said. "I've made several meatloaf sandwiches. Here's a jar of sweet cucumber pickles, a few red apples, and a whole squash pie."

"Goodness, Florence! It's supposed to be a light supper."

"And a bottle of wild grape juice," Florence continued, trying to wedge everything into the box. "Be sure and tell Carson which box is yours."

"I'll do nothing of the kind," Paula said. "And don't you tell him either."

She wrapped the box in an old slicker to conceal its identity and for protection if it should snow again.

When Paula saw Carson straddle the cow pony he had rented from the Broken Bow stables and ride away from the buildings with Eulie, she said to Florence, "Let's heat up a lot of water so I can take a bath."

"I've got enough water ready in that pot on the stove," Florence said. "I thought you might get a chance for a good wash. I put the tub behind the stove early this morning so it would be warm. I'll lock all the doors while you go upstairs and get the clothes you want to wear. Hurry before Carson gets back."

By the time Paula returned to the kitchen, Florence had pulled the curtains and locked all the outside doors. She had poured water into the large copper washtub and had placed a towel and washcloth on a chair. Florence walked into the living room and closed the door to give Paula privacy.

Paula removed her clothes and tested the water with her toe. It was a bit hot, but she knew it would cool in a hurry. She lowered her body into the tub, sat with flexed knees, and picked up a new bar of Montgomery Ward's Pure Cream Toilet Soap that she'd received through the mail a week ago. She soaped her body, careful not to get her hair wet for she wouldn't have time to dry it. She had washed her hair the day before Carson came, so it was still clean.

Sometimes Paula luxuriated in the bathwater until it became cold, but conscious of the fact that Carson might return anytime and want to come inside the house, she finished her bath quickly. She drew on a pair of black stockings, white muslin drawers with a border of Hamburg lace, and a matching cotton chemise. She put on a blue suede blouse that matched her eyes, a long, divided leather skirt, and a pair of hand-tooled leather boots. "I'm finished," she called.

Florence rustled into the kitchen, and they had all evidence of the bath removed by the time Carson returned.

nine

A strong wind was stirring the leaves of the cottonwood trees when they left for the social. Paula was wearing a long woolen cape that would drape over a saddle, but she still shivered when a blast of north wind struck her. She wore a knitted hood made of Shetland floss and tied with a black satin ribbon. Her hands were cozy in cashmere wool mitts.

Carson had on a heavy coat over his shirt and vest. His wide-brimmed hat reached his ears, and a heavy woolen muffler was wrapped around his throat. He wore a pair of gauntlet gloves embroidered with gold and cardinal silk thread. Paula thought they made a nice-looking couple.

Carson carried the box that Paula had prepared. The temperature had dropped throughout the day, and their boots crunched in the frozen snow. Shimmering rays from the moon shed light around them as they walked to the stable.

"The moonlight will make it easier to follow the trail," Paula said.

Eulie was already mounted and waiting for them in front of the bunkhouse. He had saddled Paula's pinto. She was annoyed that he was horning in on her night with Carson. "Put Daisy back in the stall." She looked at Carson. "I want to take the buckboard. It will be easier to carry my box that way. I should have asked one of the cowboys to hitch the team before they all left for the social."

"I've hitched lots of horses to buckboards," Carson said. "I'll put Daisy in the stable. Which team do you want?" he asked.

"The sorrels in the first stalls."

While Carson was in the stable, Eulie reined his horse close to Paula. "Gonna tell me what your box looks like?"

She shook her head. "That wouldn't be fair. You'll have to take a chance on your bid."

"Oh, I can probably figure it out," he said airily. "I hope Florence put in a lot of things. I'm hungry."

He seemed so confident that Paula wondered if he'd sneaked around and learned how she had wrapped the box. She hoped not. She wanted Carson to be her supper partner, but she wouldn't cheat and give him a hint.

Carson drove the buckboard team as well as he had handled the horses the day they gathered greenery to decorate the church. He obviously was a top hand, but what else did she know about him?

"Looks like you know your way around a ranch and how to handle horses," she commented.

"I've always liked working with animals. In spite of opposition from my father, I started working on the ranch when I was a kid."

"What's he got against ranching?"

"He has a mercantile business in Kansas City, and he wants me to manage it. I tried it for a couple of years, but that's not the work for me. I've told him that I will not work in the city, but I haven't convinced him."

Paula had dared to think that Carson might make a good mate, although she shouldn't have romantic thoughts about a man she had known only a few days. If he took over his father's business in Kansas City, and she inherited the Lazy R, it was doubtful she would ever see him again after the revival ended and he went home. *God forgive me! Why can't I have more faith? I know You will take care of me no matter what happens.*

Although Eulie didn't join their conversation, he stayed abreast of the buckboard as the horses quickly covered the distance to the schoolhouse. While Carson tied the team to the fence, Eulie came to Paula and helped her down from the buckboard. He then picked up the box she'd placed behind the seat.

"I'll see she gets in the schoolhouse, Hartley," Eulie said.

"Thanks. I'm going to cover the horses," Carson said, picking up blankets he had brought from the stable.

"No use of that," Eulie commented. "The horses are used to fending for themselves."

Ignoring Eulie's remark, Carson continued to see to the comfort of the animals.

Paula hurried into the schoolhouse without waiting for Eulie. Grace's twenty students must have brought all their families and friends, for the sod schoolhouse was crowded when they entered. A young man stood and insisted that Paula take his place on a bench. Eulie handed Paula's box to Grace, who stored it behind a blanket hanging in the front of the room that concealed all of the boxes. Eulie joined the men standing along the walls. She scanned the group quickly to see if the Hannson family was present, but she didn't see any of them.

Gatherings of this sort were so rare during the winter that everyone within traveling distance usually showed up. Paula noticed several young men from Broken Bow had made the long, cold ride to have the privilege of buying a girl's box and taking her home afterward. The hubbub of voices had reached such a high level that it was difficult to talk to anyone, so Paula just waved to those she knew.

She glanced around the schoolhouse that had once been the dwelling of a homesteader. Lacking wood, rock, and brick clay, the early settlers had resorted to cutting the soil into blocks, which they laid like giant bricks, then filled the cracks with loose soil to form the walls of their homes. They bought windows and doors, as well as rafters to support the heavy roofs also made of sod. The homesteader who had erected this building must have had a family, for the schoolhouse was larger than most of the early sod homes.

After the school was organized, parents had built crude desks and benches for the students. But for tonight, the desks had been removed to accommodate the large number of people who had come to the social.

A stove warmed the building, and Paula took off her heavy cape. When Carson entered, he surveyed the crowded room, flashed Paula a smile, and stood along the wall. Soon after they had arrived, Grace called everyone to attention and asked Carson to lead them in prayer.

The program started when the two youngest children, dressed like elves, began the program with short recitations of welcome.

One boy, not yet in his teens, walked to the stage wearing his cap. His parents were Irish immigrants, and with a heavy accent, he recited:

> "When Santa asked me for my name,
>   Down at the store, I said,
> 'My father calls me Sorrel-Top
>   Because my hair is red.

My mother calls me Robert,
    My grandma calls me Joy,
My grandpa calls me Bub, sometimes,
    But I call myself a boy.
Santa smiled, took off my hat,
    Looked at me, and said,
'I understand it all, my boy,
    And I shall call you Red.' "

When the boy spoke the last line, he pulled off his cap to reveal a heavy mop of auburn hair. The audience applauded heartily, which embarrassed the boy, and his face turned as red as his hair.

Every student had a part in the program, depending upon his or her age and ability. Paula was amazed that Grace, with the small amount of books she had, was able to teach the children anything. Because there were more Bibles than any other books in the community, she used them for textbooks, and the program concluded with a monologue by one of the older girls portraying Mary, the mother of Jesus.

Wrapped in a white blanket, the girl skillfully related the appearance of the angel who told Mary that she would become the mother of Jesus. She spoke of her days of doubt, the mistreatment she received from her friends in Nazareth while she waited for the birth of God's Son, and the anguish she experienced when her Son was nailed to the cross. Lifting her folded hands upward, she concluded, "My Son was born to die and become the Savior of the world. If you haven't accepted the message of salvation He brought and received God's Son into your heart, Christmas has no meaning for you."

After the program ended in this reverent manner, Grace said, "Now, everybody close your eyes while we arrange the boxes to be auctioned off. No peeking."

This was the moment Paula dreaded. At the last social she'd attended, Eulie had bought her box, but the previous time, a Swedish homesteader had been the purchaser. A man in his midfifties, he knew only a few words of English, and he ate so rapidly that Paula wondered how long it had been since he'd had enough to eat. She had insisted that he take her portion, also. Since it was customary for the person who bought the box to escort the lady home, Paula feared it would be an ordeal, but as it turned out, Mr. Sanderson had had no means of transportation except walking. It was quite a distance to the Lazy R, so he didn't ask to take her home. But what would happen tonight?

A rancher who was also an auctioneer at livestock sales came forward to accept the bids. Grace held up a box wrapped in a piece of calico tied with a string of tinsel. The first offering always brought a flurry of bids, as the younger boys tried to buy a box with the few pennies they had. The men usually humored the boys and let them take the bids unless they thought the box happened to belong to their chosen ladies.

As the bidding continued and her contribution wasn't offered, Paula became more and more agitated. Her box was the last one offered for sale. Paula clenched her hands to keep them from trembling. She tried to compose her features so no one could tell by her expression that the box was hers, but her face must have deceived her for Eulie jumped into the bidding by calling out, "One dollar," which was a large amount to start a bid.

Money was scarce in Custer County, and two dollars

was usually the highest bid on any box at a social. Another cowboy increased the bid by a quarter, and Eulie quickly raised his offer to two dollars. When the auctioneer began the countdown that would give Eulie the box, Carson startled Paula by calling out, "Three dollars!"

Quick bidding swung back and forth between the two men, each raising the amount by fifty cents until Carson reached ten dollars. "Ten dollars once!" the auctioneer called out. "Ten dollars twice! Ten dollars three times!" The auctioneer looked to Eulie, but he just shook his head. The auctioneer banged his gavel. "Sold to Mr. Hartley for ten dollars!"

Eulie slammed his fist against the wall. "Preachin' must be payin' good these days," he muttered.

As Carson went forward to claim Paula's box, Eulie stomped out of the schoolhouse, slamming the door. Paula buried her flaming face in her hands. She'd never been so mortified in her life, and she didn't know which one to blame the most—Carson or Eulie.

Although no one in the building could have believed otherwise, Grace announced that the box belonged to Paula. She handed the box to Carson, adding complacently, "How grateful I am for such a nice bid. Remember that the proceeds from this sale will buy Christmas treats for the schoolchildren, and if we get enough money, we'll provide food baskets to take home to their families. All receipts, large or small, are appreciated."

Knowing how bleak Christmas would be for some of these children, Paula tried to ignore her own embarrassment, for Carson's high bid *would* do a lot of good. She had suspected that Carson came from a wealthy family, for his clothes, while not new, were obviously of high quality. His father being a Kansas City merchant, as well as the owner of a ranch, indicated that Carson could afford to spend ten dollars. So she decided to forget her embarrassment and enjoy the evening. She would deal with Eulie's anger later. She'd had about enough of his jealousy anyway, especially since she hadn't given him any encouragement.

Grace clapped her hands when the money was counted and totaled over thirty dollars. "Thank you so much," she said. "Your Christmas will be merrier now that you've provided for others. And since it is the Christmas season, it would be nice if those of you who were successful in bidding will share with others."

"Good idea," Carson said as he took a seat beside Paula. "Gather around," he called out with a sweeping gesture to the crowd.

While he divided the contents of the box into small portions and placed them in outstretched hands, he said quietly to Paula. "I'm sorry I embarrassed you, but since I considered you were my girl for the night, I didn't like it when Eulie horned in." With a grimace, he added, "That's a poor attitude for a preacher to have, but I think God will forgive me for He knows how much I want to spend the evening with you."

His remarks flustered Paula, and she felt her face coloring. She couldn't think of anything to say, so she picked up a red apple and started nibbling on it.

By ten o'clock, the food was gone, and sleeping children were curled like cocoons in their blankets and spread out on the floor of the schoolhouse. Carson wrapped Paula's empty box in the slicker and placed her cape around her shoulders. When they reached the buckboard, Paula stopped suddenly. "One horse is gone!"

"So it is," Carson said, not sounding the least bit surprised.

"Who could have stolen it?"

"I'm sure the horse will be safe in its own stall when we get back to the Lazy R. I expected Eulie to seek revenge because I outbid him for your box."

"But how are we going to get home?" Paula stammered in bewilderment.

"With one animal gone, Eulie thought you'd ride the remaining horse, and that I'd have to walk. Maybe we can outwit Eulie at his own game. Since I don't intend to take a long walk tonight, do you mind riding double?"

Paula was glad the moonlight concealed her embarrassment, for she felt her face flaming. "It won't be very comfortable," she stammered.

"True, but you can sit sideways on the horse as if you had a sidesaddle, and I'll ride behind you. That horse is strong enough to carry both of us," Carson argued.

Grace and the Schultzes came out of the schoolhouse at that time. Grace said, "I thought you'd be gone by now."

"We ran into some trouble—one of the buckboard horses has disappeared," Carson said.

Mr. Schultz held up his lantern.

Grace shot a quick glance toward Paula, and she said, "Eulie! That was a dirty trick." Under her breath, she said, "It's time you gave him his walking papers."

Paula didn't answer. What could she say? She wasn't sure she had the authority to fire the foreman.

"Come by our house, and we'll loan you a horse," Mr. Schultz offered.

"No, that's quite a distance out of our way," Paula refused. "We can both ride the same horse."

Grace stood close to her, and she poked Paula in the

ribs. "Good idea," she whispered. "This is a great night for a moonlight ride." Paula frowned at her grinning friend.

The Lazy R cowboys who had attended the social gathered around them, but they remained noncommittal about what had happened. They probably knew that they would pay for it if they said anything against the foreman.

Carson unhitched the horse, put the harness in the buckboard, and placed a folded blanket behind the saddle. He leaped astride the blanket and reached down for Paula as Schultz and Grace pushed her upward. When she was settled in front of him, Carson put his arms around her and lifted the reins. The horse started forward when Carson gave it a gentle kick in the side. They rode mostly in silence, and after a few miles, Paula relaxed against Carson's chest. His arms tightened, and he pulled her close. This was the first time Paula had ever been held in a man's arms, and she decided she liked it.

When they reached the Lazy R, the other sorrel was in its stall, as Carson had predicted, but any confrontation he might have had with Eulie was postponed because the Lazy R cowboys, who'd been at the social, cantered into the barnyard soon after he stabled the mare. The moon was now overhead, casting deep shadows around the yard as Paula and Carson walked to the ranch house.

"In spite of Eulie's meanness," Paula said, "I've enjoyed the evening, but I'm sorry you had an uncomfortable ride coming home."

"Not at all," Carson said with a low chuckle as he opened the door. "That was the best part of the whole evening."

Paula's face grew warm. One lamp, with its flame turned low, lighted the room, and a faint glow came from the fireplace that Florence had already banked for the night.

She was glad Carson couldn't see how flustered she was.

At the top of the stairs, Paula turned toward her own room, but Carson halted her with his hand on her shoulder. Bending forward, he kissed her lightly on the forehead. Paula gasped and scurried down the hallway.

She shut the door of her room and leaned against it, trembling all over. Why did this have to happen to her now? Her frustration over losing the Lazy R was trouble enough. Why did she have to get involved romantically with a man she hardly knew? Could this be love? How else could she explain the contentment she'd experienced tonight when she'd nestled so close in Carson's arms that she felt his heart beat?

She shivered, more from excitement than cold, as she hastily slipped into a flannel nightgown and got into bed. In times like these, she missed her mother acutely. Florence was good to her, but she didn't have much patience with a young woman's "vapors," as she called Paula's frustrations. With Florence, every issue was either "black or white." She didn't trust Eulie; therefore, he wasn't a suitable companion for Paula. Carson, on the other hand, was a preacher and trustworthy, so her friend had decided that Carson would be a good husband for Paula. But did Carson's attentions indicate marriage?

Paula left her warm bed long enough to kneel in prayer. "God, I want to do what's right. First, forgive me for my uncompromising attitude about Frank Randall. The Lazy R belonged to Dad. If he wanted his nephew to have it, that was his decision to make. If I inherit the ranch and Carson asked me to marry him, the property would be a problem, so perhaps it will be better for me if the nephew does inherit it. I've got to stop dreading Randall's homecoming.

If he comes, help me to be gracious about my loss and guide me into the future You have for me. I pray for Your forgiveness and Your guidance. Amen."

Settling back into bed under the warm comforters, Paula wished she knew what Carson *really* thought of her.

&

In his room, Carson was also on his knees praying for God's guidance. For several years, his parents had been pressuring him to marry, and he'd always intended to take a wife someday. Had "someday" finally arrived? Had he known Paula too short a time to make a decision about her? Probably so, for her connection with Eulie Benedict and her attitude about Gordon Randall's will bothered him.

"Our Father in heaven," he prayed after much soul-searching, "there's a cloud between us. I can't determine Your will in this matter. Is this one of the times when I have to act in faith without having the complete blueprint of what the future holds?"

As he settled into Gordon Randall's bed, he thought for a long time about the man who had once occupied this room.

ten

At breakfast the next morning, Paula was embarrassed and her hands fumbled. She dropped her fork, and Florence brought a clean one. Then she spilled coffee on her plate.

Florence's eyes darted from Carson to Paula, and never one to ignore an issue, she demanded, "What happened last night to make you so edgy?"

Carson picked up a biscuit and buttered it. Paula's napkin slipped off her lap onto the floor, and she bent to retrieve it.

"Who bought your box?" Florence persisted.

"I was the lucky bidder," Carson said, coming to Paula's rescue.

"And what did Eulie think about that?"

"Oh, Florence, stop pestering us. You know how Eulie is. He was madder than an old wet hen."

"I'll have a talk with Eulie before I leave today," Carson said, "so there's no need for either of you to fret about it."

Apparently assuming that Eulie's anger had been the only cause for Paula's uneasiness, Florence asked no more questions. Paula got her emotions in check before the meal ended, and putting a shawl over her shoulders, she walked out on the porch in the crisp morning air to say good-bye to Carson.

He took her hands in his strong grasp. "I apologize for being so forward last night," he said. His smile made her feel as if she were wrapped in invisible warmth. "I've wanted to kiss you since the first day I met you."

When she wouldn't look at him, Carson put a hand under her chin and lifted her gaze to his. "I didn't mean to insult you."

"I didn't consider it an insult. I was surprised and didn't know what to do."

He grinned. "It would have been pleasant if you'd kissed me back. Do you want to return the favor before I go?"

Paula had seldom blushed before she met Carson, and now much to her disgust, her face flamed. "Not in daylight!"

Carson laughed softly—a sound that Paula found most pleasant. "I was only joking. But I'm not dallying with you, Paula. After I do some thinking and praying, we must have a serious talk. Is that all right with you?"

"Yes. But as you know, everything in my life is on hold until Christmas Day."

"I understand that." He lifted her hand and kissed her fingers. "I'll confront Eulie and go back to town. When will I see you again?"

"Grace told me last night that Reverend Bailey wants to meet next week to prepare Christmas treats and practice some music for the Christmas Eve service. If the weather holds, I plan to come to town for that."

"Then I'll look forward to seeing you at that time."

❧

Carson's face set grimly as he headed toward the out-buildings. He didn't welcome a confrontation with Eulie, but he couldn't overlook the man's behavior last night. Eulie was standing in the doorway as Carson led his horse out of the stall.

To his surprise, Eulie was smiling. He reached a hand to Carson. "Reverend, I want to apologize for my actions last night. I'm not a bit proud of the way I acted—like a jealous, lovesick boy."

Carson shook his hand and released it, but he didn't say anything. What had brought about Eulie's change of attitude?

"Fact is, Preacher, you were overstepping your bounds a little. After all, me and Paula are going to marry, and by rights, I should have gotten her box at the social."

His words startled Carson, but he tried to suppress his reaction. "You didn't have to stop bidding."

Eulie grinned sheepishly. "I wasn't expecting the biddin' to go so high, and that's all the money I took with me."

"When are you and Paula planning to marry?"

"We haven't set the date yet. But when Paula inherits this ranch, she'll need a husband to take care of it for her, so it'll be soon."

"I've understood that she doesn't have first claim to the ranch. Will you still want to marry Paula if Randall's nephew comes to claim the ranch?"

Eulie's dark face took on a vicious expression. "He won't show up. And if he does, he won't last long around here."

Carson stepped into the saddle and lifted his hand in parting. He didn't intend to apologize to Eulie for "overstepping his bounds." He thought the foreman was lying, but if he wasn't, the only thing he could do as a gentleman was to bow out and let them continue their courtship. Perhaps he should avoid Paula until after the revival, and then he'd leave the country. He was half-tempted to stop at the ranch house and ask Paula if she had promised to marry Eulie, for he couldn't help but believe that she would have told him if she intended to marry Eulie.

❧

As Carson passed the ranch house, Paula stepped out on the porch and waved to him. She had witnessed the exchange between Eulie and Carson, fearing that Eulie would physically attack the man he considered his rival. It surprised her that their exchange had seemed amiable when she had expected a fistfight, or even worse. Carson was wearing his six-shooter, as he had when they were riding the range on Friday. She had a feeling that he didn't carry the weapon for show, and in spite of all his bullying, Eulie was a poor shot.

Watching Carson's broad shoulders as he rode away, she wondered again at his attentions to her. Could his knowledge that she was a potential owner of thousands of acres of prime Nebraska rangeland have influenced his friendliness?

There I go again! she scolded herself. It was true that Carson's interest in her did seem sudden. But she'd only known him a short time, and she suspected that she was falling in love with *him*. So couldn't it work both ways?

Paula had never been so confused in her life, and the only antidote she knew for the distraction was work. Going into the kitchen, she said, "Florence, I'm worried about the immigrant family living in that old dugout. I don't suppose they have much to eat. What can I do to help them without Eulie finding out? If I take food to them, he might follow me."

"Didn't Grace mention they were sending their kids to school?"

"Yes, but they weren't at the social last night."

"We could fix up a box of food and have Grace give it to the children."

"That's a good idea. And I'll buy some gifts for the family when I go to Broken Bow. Perhaps we can go visit them on Christmas Day and take their presents."

"It's time we start baking for Christmas anyway. I'll cook mincemeat today, and we can make pies tomorrow," Florence said.

"On Monday, I'll bake a pan of corn bread for the Hannsons and take it and a couple of jars of plum jam to Grace. If the children aren't at school, she won't mind leaving it at the dugout when she goes home. I need to stay busy to keep my mind off my problems."

❧

As he cantered along the trail, Carson evaluated the worth of the Lazy R spread. He knew that the price of livestock fluctuated to a great extent, but even considering that, he believed the Randall ranch, if handled right, could be a prosperous one. But was Eulie Benedict capable of managing a ranch of this magnitude? He swung aside from the trail to look at a herd of Herefords that bore the Lazy R brand and came face-to-face with a man he'd seen at the Inman Hotel. He was riding a horse from the livery stable in town.

"Howdy!" Carson said, wondering why the man was on Lazy R property. "Are you heading toward the ranch headquarters?"

The man shook his head. "No, just looking over the country."

"Figuring to settle here?" Carson asked, knowing he was breaking a cardinal rule of the West by quizzing a man about his personal business. But he had Paula's interests at heart, and he wondered if the word was out that Frank Randall couldn't be found and pseudoclaimants were arriving with an eye on taking the ranch.

"I don't know. Are you?"

Carson laughed, knowing that the man resented his questions. "You can't ever tell. I might," he said, lifting the reins and continuing on his way. Although he didn't trust Eulie, the other Lazy R cowboys had impressed Carson. For the time being, he decided he would let them look after Paula's interests. Besides, Carson Hartley, born Frank Carson Randall, had much to occupy his mind. He couldn't remember his biological father, who had died when Carson was two years old. When his mother married Ira Hartley, Ira had adopted Carson legally and changed his name. He was fond of his stepfather, although Carson had often wished that he could have kept the Randall name. But Ira was jealous of his wife, and he didn't want their son's name to remind him of her first husband.

As he rode slowly, no longer admiring the landscape, Carson thought of the events that had led to his arrival in Broken Bow. When the letter from Homer Sullivan had finally reached Carson, he had never seen his father so angry. Ira considered Carson's legacy a snag in his plans to have his son take over his mercantile company.

Although Carson's mother didn't usually oppose her strong-willed husband, this time she took a stand. "Carson is a grown man, Ira. Stop treating him like a child. If he's inclined to manage your business, inheriting a ranch in Nebraska isn't going to stop him. There's nothing you can do to alter the fact that our son was born a Randall, and if he wants to follow in the steps of his father's relatives, let him make the decision."

Relenting, Ira helped him make the necessary preparations for his journey and sent Carson off with a pat on the back and a handshake. Carson had always respected his father's opinions, and he wished that Ira were here now to help him sort out his muddled thoughts. He should have told Paula right away that he was Gordon's nephew. If he told her now, she would be angry, and he wouldn't blame her. But should he even tell her? If she wanted to marry Eulie Benedict, he would let them have the ranch. When he would eventually inherit the considerable Hartley holdings in Kansas, he wouldn't need the ranch, but he hesitated to leave without telling her. In spite of the addendum to the will, as long as Gordon's nephew was alive, that could pose a threat to her ownership of the ranch.

He believed in living by the Golden Rule—to treat others as he'd want to be treated. He didn't want Eulie Benedict to marry Paula, but if he were engaged to a girl, he wouldn't want another man to take her away from him. Paula acted like she was interested in him, but had she deceived him and *was* planning to marry Eulie?

"God, I love her, and I'm not too objective in my decisions. Like Gideon, I'm putting out the fleece. Please give me a sign so I'll know if I should try to win her love."

Before he went to bed that night, Carson read one of his favorite scriptures from Psalm 37: "Delight thyself also in the LORD; and he shall give thee the desires of thine heart. Commit thy way unto the LORD; trust also in him; and he shall bring it to pass." The past few days in Paula's presence had convinced him that she was the desire of his heart, so he slept soundly, believing that God would guide him.

eleven

Carson had walked by Homer Sullivan's office several times since his arrival in Broken Bow, wondering if he should go in. Today was the day. Shortly after nine o'clock, Carson walked into the lawyer's waiting room. The door into the inner office was ajar, and Carson knocked on the doorjamb.

"Come in," a deep voice summoned, and Carson went into the lawyer's office and shut the door behind him. The middle-aged Sullivan stood and shook hands with Carson and invited him to sit down. "What can I do for you?" he asked, obviously assessing Carson through bifocal spectacles set in a steel frame.

Carson took a packet of papers from his inner pocket. He handed Sullivan the letter the lawyer had written to Frank Randall, a letter of identification from a prominent lawyer in Kansas City, proof of his adoption by Ira Hartley, and a legal document showing that he was the son of Gordon Randall's only brother.

Sullivan carefully read the papers twice before he leaned back in his chair, took off his spectacles, and laid them on the desk in front of him. His expressive gray eyes twinkled in amusement. "It's a big surprise to learn that the much-talked-of Cowboy Preacher is heir to the Lazy R Ranch. Why have you concealed your identity?"

Carson hesitated slightly. "Father's lawyer advised me to travel incognito and look over the situation before

85

I revealed who I was. Then I met Paula Thompson on the train when I was coming to Broken Bow. She told me about the addendum to the will, which you hadn't mentioned in your letter, and I didn't want to say anything until I learned more about the situation."

"But you *are* the Cowboy Preacher?"

"Yes, of course. I wouldn't lie about that. After I talked with Reverend Bailey, I decided that God had a two-fold purpose for my coming to Broken Bow—to check on the Lazy R situation *and* also to preach the gospel in this town."

"We're expecting great things from the revival."

"There will be if God is glorified by what I say. I'm only a cowboy the Lord called to preach."

Sullivan pointed to the papers on his desk. "But a little more than a cowboy, I'd judge. I've heard of Hartley Mercantile Enterprises. I doubt you're a pauper."

"That belongs to my father. I manage his ranch for him, but I work for wages like the rest of the hands. I prefer it that way."

"It looks to me as if you're qualified to take over the Lazy R. Gordon was a cowman—he turned that area into a prime piece of real estate."

"I agree. I took advantage of my slight acquaintance with Miss Thompson and looked over the Lazy R. It is a fine ranch."

"One of the best in the county. But about the addendum, I didn't know about it when I wrote to you. It didn't surface until several months after Gordon died."

"So I understood. When I realized how Paula was hurting about losing her home, I didn't have the heart to tell her I was Gordon's heir. I haven't told anyone who I am, thinking if the Lazy R and this area didn't interest me, I'd disappear and leave her undisturbed. I'm not sure that I want to do that now, but just in case I do, what legal steps are necessary to give the ranch to her?"

Sullivan fidgeted in his chair, drumming on the edge of the desk with his fingers. "Are you sure you want to make that sacrifice for a girl you've only known a short time? I thought you liked the ranch." Sullivan's voice and facial expression indicated that he questioned Carson's mentality.

"I like it very much." Carson laughed lightly. "In spite of Father's determination to turn me into a merchant, I'm a rancher at heart. My first dad died without realizing his dream of owning a ranch. Perhaps I inherited his dream. Mainly, I feel it's unchristian to deprive Miss Thompson of her home, especially when I'll eventually inherit my father's wealth."

Sullivan closed his eyes, and Carson wondered if he was taking a nap. Apparently the lawyer was deep in thought, though, for his eyes snapped open as if he'd come to a sudden decision.

"You may change your mind about that." He pushed his chair back from the desk, stood to his six-foot height, and strolled to a massive vault in the corner of the room. Squinting, he turned the combination lock, opened the door, and withdrew a large envelope. He laid the envelope on the desk, and Carson saw that it was labeled RANDALL ESTATE. He handed Carson the handwritten will of Gordon Randall. The words were simple and brief, leaving his entire estate to Frank C. Randall, the son of his brother; last-known residence, Colorado Territory.

"That will was witnessed by two reputable men who still live in Custer County, so they can testify to Randall's signature. The last letter Gordon had from your mother told him that his brother had died, thanking him for remembering you in his will. If your mother knew you were heir to Frank's estate, why didn't she keep in touch with him?"

"My mother left Colorado and moved to Missouri after my father died. Her parents lived in Independence, and she met and married Ira Hartley when I was still a child. Ira's a good man, but because he has a possessive nature, he resented my mother's first marriage. I suppose that's why she didn't keep in contact with my uncle. She didn't tell me that I was named in his will until we received your letter."

Sullivan handed Carson another piece of paper, and he unfolded it to find the addendum to Gordon's will, dated two years ago. Carson read it aloud. " 'I haven't heard from my nephew for many years. If he can't be located within a year from the date of my death, my estate is to pass to my dearly beloved stepdaughter, Paula Thompson.' " Carson looked at the two papers and glanced at the lawyer expectantly, puzzled by his grave expression. "No one witnessed the signing of the document, which seems a little strange, but there should be enough people around here to identify it as my uncle's writing."

"Place the two papers side by side and compare them," Sullivan said, arching his fingers into a steeple in front of him.

Carson placed the will and the addendum on the desk and studied them carefully. He couldn't see anything wrong with either paper, and he wondered at Sullivan's manner. "The paper the will was written on is yellow, and the ink has faded; the addendum is neat, crisp, and the script more legible. Is that what you mean?"

"Compare the handwriting. Do you see any differences in the script?"

After studying the two papers for several minutes, Carson shook his head slowly.

"The addendum wasn't written by Gordon Randall. It's a forgery," the lawyer stated bluntly.

Carson was shocked at Sullivan's words. He raised his head quickly, staring at the other man in disbelief.

The lawyer moved around the desk to stand beside Carson, and he pointed to the two papers. "It's clever work, obviously done by a professional forger, but there are a few differences. Notice that the capital *S* is slanted toward the left in the will, but not in the addendum. Look at the apostrophes—in the will, none of them are made the same way. In the other paper, they're all alike. And the *T*s are curved differently in the first document. The addendum is a perfect script, everything as it should be. Normal writing isn't that perfect."

"But considering the number of years between the two documents, couldn't Uncle Gordon's writing have changed?" Carson asked, desperately wanting to prove that the document wasn't a forgery.

"Yes, and it may have changed, but probably not for the better. Gordon was an unlearned man, and I can't see him writing such a good paper. He was also a careful man, and if he'd written this addendum, he would have had his signature witnessed. If he'd written the document when they were on roundup, there would have been several cowhands to witness it."

"This is terrible! Whom do you suspect?"

"Paula and Eulie, of course. They're the only ones who would profit."

"I can't believe Paula is involved," Carson declared, his heartbeat accelerating. "It must have been Eulie." He'd asked God for a sign, but he hadn't expected this.

"Paula brought it to me."

"Yes, but she said the foreman had found it. If they had it forged, why would they have given a year's leeway for my return?"

"I've wondered about that," Sullivan admitted. "But they probably decided it would arouse people's suspicions if you weren't mentioned at all. Randall talked about you quite a lot, wondering if he would ever see you again, and it wasn't like him to cut you out altogether."

"What about this man. . .this Roscoe McCoy who's hanging around town? Maybe he and Eulie are in cahoots to steal the ranch." Carson knew he was grasping at straws to disprove Paula's involvement.

Sullivan resumed his seat across the desk from Carson. "If that's so, Eulie wouldn't get the ranch. If he marries Paula, he'll have what he's been coveting for several years. Gordon told me once that Eulie had aspirations, although he didn't spell out what he meant. He probably realized that Eulie would try to marry Paula to get hold of the Lazy R, and that's the reason he didn't change his will to include her. I never did think Gordon liked his foreman, and I often wondered why he didn't get rid of him."

"Paula seems to think he's a good cowman."

"That's true—and they aren't easy to find—but I was determined that he wouldn't get his hands on the Randall ranch. So I made a trip to Omaha in October, and I had a handwriting expert take a look at the two documents. He agrees that the same person did not write them. Since my suspicions were vindicated, I haven't done anything. I've been hoping Frank Randall would show up and I wouldn't have to make the decision. I've always been fond of Paula, and I don't want to cause her any trouble. I want to believe that Eulie has deceived her. The decision is up to you now."

"Thanks," Carson said with laughter that held no amusement. He shook his head, hoping to dispel the gloom that surrounded him. Surely Paula wasn't a crook! Or was that why she was so nervous about the situation— fearing that her crime would be detected? "Will you give me a few days to think about this? If Eulie alone is responsible, I want him punished, but. . ."

"I understand," Sullivan said, and from the compassion in his eyes, Carson thought the lawyer did recognize his inward struggle. "And it may be that Eulie is the only culprit. I do know that a few weeks before the addendum surfaced, Eulie went to Lincoln and was gone for three days."

He reached in a desk drawer and withdrew a Lincoln newspaper. Tapping a short article, he handed it to Carson. "This article indicates that a forger was recently arrested in the capital city. He's been found guilty of writing counterfeit wills, deeds, and other documents. I'm going to Lincoln on Thursday to talk to the man. Do you want to come with me?"

"Absolutely!"

"I found a picture of Gordon, Paula, and Eulie taken in 1886, the day the first train came to Broken Bow. That's been a few years, but Eulie hasn't changed much since then. I'll take it along for identification."

Carson left the lawyer's office with a heavy heart. Had he finally found the woman he wanted to marry, only to discover she was in cahoots with another man to rob him of his birthright?

twelve

The weather was fair on Thursday, and Paula persuaded Florence to go with her to Broken Bow. They made plans to stay overnight and help prepare treats for those who came to the Christmas Eve service and baskets for the town's needy families. Florence stayed with her daughter, but Paula took a room at the Inman Hotel. She looked eagerly for Carson when she went to the dining room for supper. When he didn't put in an appearance, she thought he would surely be at the church.

A large group of people gathered to fill brown paper bags with hard candies and other treats. Paula helped fill several baskets with canned goods, potatoes, and dried beans, which Reverend Bailey would take to indigent families a few days before Christmas. Paula kept watching the door, expecting Carson to show up. During the two hours the group worked, Carson didn't arrive and his name wasn't mentioned. As everyone prepared to leave, Paula approached Reverend Bailey.

"Mr. Hartley said that he would be here tonight."

"He's gone away for a few days. I saw him at the railway station this morning with Homer Sullivan, but he assured me that he would return before Christmas Eve. I've asked him to help with the service."

Paula was embarrassed to be asking questions about Carson, but she would be miserable until she found out where he was. "Did he go back to Kansas City?"

"No. He told me he was going to Lincoln."

Her pride wouldn't permit Paula to ask any more questions, but she was puzzled. When he left the Lazy R on Sunday, Carson hadn't been planning a trip. Or had he? And why had he gone with Mr. Sullivan?

Paula spent a miserable night, turning back and forth in the bed, wishing she knew more about Carson.

The next morning, Paula wasn't enthusiastic about buying Christmas gifts, especially when she went into the Central Nebraska Bank to withdraw some cash and realized that her small hoard of money was almost gone. Mentally, she counted the few remaining days until Christmas. When that day arrived, she would either be a pauper or prosperous. She was tempted not to buy any gifts for the Hannsons, but a verse from the Bible entered her mind unbidden: "Inasmuch as ye have done it unto one of the least of these my brethren, ye have done it unto me."

Remembering the scared, pinched faces of the two children in the dugout, at Salisbury Dry Goods Store, she bought sweaters for them and a doll for the girl. At Ryerson & Leslie's Books and Stationery, she purchased a picture book for the boy and a novel for Florence. She had bought shirts for the Lazy R cowboys in Grand Island that she'd used Lazy R funds for, as Mr. Sullivan agreed that would be a legitimate expense for the ranch.

❧

Paula and Florence returned to the ranch the next day, and it took all of Paula's willpower to get out of bed the following morning. She wasn't hungry, and at breakfast, she sipped at a cup of coffee and nibbled on a biscuit. Florence helped herself to a second serving of biscuits and gravy before she said, "What's the matter with you? You're acting like a lovesick kid. Just because Carson left town for a few days doesn't mean he won't come back."

Stung by Florence's words, Paula said angrily, "I am not lovesick. I'm worried. Why did he and Mr. Sullivan go away together? That's what I'd like to know."

Florence snorted. "Maybe they didn't go together. It might have been a coincidence that they took the same train."

Paula shook her head. "I've tried to tell myself that, but the last time I went to see Mr. Sullivan, he wasn't very kind to me. Maybe he's heard from Frank Randall and won't tell me."

"What you need is a little more faith in your Maker and a lot less fretting about things you can't help. If Frank Randall comes to claim this ranch, you'll have to accept it. You know what Paul said in the book of Romans: 'All things work together for good to them that love God, to them who are the called according to his purpose.' You belong to God. He'll take care of you."

At that inopportune time, Eulie opened the door and rushed into the kitchen. His face was as black as a thunderhead.

"Why did you tell those squatters they could stay on the Lazy R?"

Having Florence criticize her was bad enough, but she wasn't in the mood for a tongue-lashing from Eulie. Paula pushed back her chair so fast it overturned, and she turned stormy blue eyes on the foreman.

"Because they need a home. What have you done to them?"

"I haven't done anything to them, yet, but I'm taking the cowhands to drive them off the ranch."

"No! They've been living there for a month, and if you'd been tending to your work, you'd have discovered them before I did."

"Seems like there are lots of things you haven't told me. Why did Hartley and Sullivan leave town together?"

"I have no idea, but it's none of my business, or yours either."

"And that's where you might be wrong," he said, slamming the door as he left the kitchen.

Paula shuddered. "To think I've actually wondered if I should marry that man," she said. "What will I do if I inherit the ranch? I can't have Eulie badgering me like this, but I don't have the courage to fire him."

"He wouldn't leave anyway," Florence said, as she took dishes from the table and immersed them in a pan of hot, sudsy water. "You need a husband to help you run this ranch. He can deal with Eulie."

With a slight grin, Paula said, "Do you have anyone in mind?"

"Yes, the same one you do."

"I can't make any plans until I know if the ranch belongs to me, and then I'll decide on the future. When Eulie acts like he did this morning, I'd just as soon Frank Randall would come and relieve me of the responsibility." She jerked a towel from the rack behind the stove, and as she wiped the dishes that Florence rinsed, she said, "Jesus told His followers not to worry about tomorrow, that the things of tomorrow would take care of themselves, and that we should seek the kingdom of God. I'm going to put that in practice today and go see the Hannsons. I'd appreciate it if you'd come with me. I want to be sure that Eulie hasn't evicted them."

"We'll take some food. I'll make a spice cake while you go to the cellar and get some potatoes and a few jars of vegetables—something they can heat up easily."

"Grace said the children don't have much to eat," Paula said, her spirits lifting. "And we might take some of our extra comforters. That dugout must be cold. I've hesitated to do anything to help them because I didn't want Eulie to know they were there."

"Are you going to take their Christmas gifts?"

"Not today."

"Good. I'm knitting caps for the children, and I don't have them finished."

With this purpose in mind, Paula threw off the lethargy of the past few days. They waited until after lunch before Paula went to the bunkhouse and asked one of the cowboys to hitch the horses to the buckboard and bring it to the house. He offered to drive for her, but there wasn't much snow on the ground now, and she could manage all right.

When they rode down the valley to the dugout, Paula was relieved to see smoke coming from the stovepipe stuck through the roof of the sod house. At least Eulie hadn't put them out yet! When they stopped the buckboard, the man came out carrying a shotgun, which he laid aside when he saw the two women.

"Mr. Hannson," Paula said, "I've brought my friend to see your wife. Florence is good with sick people, and she may be able to help her."

She tied the horses, and Florence climbed out of the buckboard.

"We also brought some food. Will you help me carry these things into the dugout?"

Mr. Hannson took the food containers, and Paula and

Florence walked before him into the shack.

The children had evidently gone to school, for no one was in the house except a fair, wan woman lying on a pallet of ragged quilts near the stove, so rusty that the fire could be seen through holes in the metal. Surprisingly, the room didn't feel as damp as Paula had thought it would.

"I'm Paula Thompson, and this is my friend, Florence. She'll help you."

The woman shook her head and turned questioning eyes on her husband.

"Britta is vith child."

Paula took another look at the woman, and even in the dim light, it was evident that Mrs. Hannson was indeed expecting a child.

"You two go on outside. I want to examine her," Florence instructed.

"She does not speak the English," Mr. Hannson explained.

"She doesn't need to speak English. This will be woman talk—the same in all languages!" With a shooing gesture, she herded Paula and Mr. Hannson toward the door. He pulled the skin aside, and they went outside, staying close to the dugout to avoid the wind.

"The cowboy come," Hannson said. "He angry, order us to leave, but ven I show him your note, he vent away, but still angry."

"That was the Lazy R foreman, and I've told him to leave you alone." Paula added, "I hope he does."

Several minutes later, Florence joined them, a smile on her face.

"Your wife is fine, Mr. Hannson, and you should have a fine baby in a couple of weeks. You're not to worry." After she and Paula climbed into the buckboard, Florence said, "Your wife will know the time to send for me." She pointed northward. "You ride in that direction to reach the Lazy R headquarters."

Hannson took Florence's hand and pumped it up and down.

"Tank you," he said. "So vorried—didn't know how I could manage."

"You have friends now, Mr. Hannson," Paula assured him. As she trotted the horses back to the ranch house, she said, "There's nothing like helping other people to take your mind off your own problems. I feel a 100 percent better than I did this morning."

thirteen

Carson and Sullivan made the trip back from Lincoln almost in silence. Their suspicions had been confirmed, and neither man knew what to do with their findings. They'd visited the convicted forger in jail, and he readily admitted that he'd forged the counterfeit addendum. With only one glance at Eulie's photo, he identified him as the man who'd paid him a hundred dollars to write the paper. He had no idea whether or not Paula was involved in the incident. And, saying that one more crime wouldn't make any difference in his sentence, he signed a confession admitting that Eulie had hired him to forge the document.

The train car was empty except for the two of them after they left Grand Island. Breaking the silence, Carson said, "I don't know what to do."

"There's one thing for sure: I won't let Eulie Benedict get his hands on the Lazy R," the lawyer said. "But I won't make my move until you come to a decision."

"I still can't believe Paula had anything to do with this. But even if she did, I don't want her sent to prison. Losing the Lazy R will be punishment enough."

"You're in love with her, aren't you?" Sullivan said when the train whistle announced their arrival at the town of Berwyn.

"I suppose so. I never believed that there was any such thing as love at first sight, but I'm beginning to think it can happen. It's not a comforting feeling. I've waited a long time to fall in love, and now I've settled on a woman who might be trying to steal my inheritance. It's unbelievable!"

"I sympathize with you, but I can't overlook the situation. If you won't, I'm going to turn this information over to the authorities."

"I understand your position," Carson assured him, "but will you give me a few days before you do anything?"

"The prisoner didn't make any secret about what he had done, and there was a reporter hanging around. The newspapers will soon get hold of the story. You won't have much time to make up your mind."

"Please don't tell anyone who I am. I want to be the one to tell Paula."

The difficult situation still plagued Carson after they arrived in Broken Bow and he went to his hotel room. Indecision and anxiety drove him to his knees, where he spent most of the night. What would Jesus do in a similar situation? Christ was the most compassionate person who'd ever walked on earth, but He didn't allow iniquity to go unpunished. "He that doeth wrong shall receive for the wrong which he hath done: and there is no respect of persons." Carson had often used that Bible verse from Paul's letter to the Colossians in his messages.

If Paula was guilty, she should be punished as well as Eulie. Although his faith had wavered, Carson still didn't believe that she was involved. The foreman must have had the will forged, and she was so happy to know her stepfather had remembered her that she hadn't questioned the windfall.

Carson finally slept a few hours, but he had gotten up and was shaving the next morning when heavy steps sounded in the hallway, followed by a persistent knocking on his door. "Come in," he invited and turned his lathered face as Sullivan hurriedly entered the room. Swiping a towel across his face, Carson asked, "What's wrong?"

"Several people in town, including me, subscribe to Lincoln newspapers. A packet of them arrived on last night's train. The forger's trial made the front page. He admitted counterfeiting the Randall addendum as one of his crimes. The sheriff came to my house this morning to see what I knew. I had to admit that I'd talked to the man."

"You didn't say anything about me?" When Sullivan shook his head, Carson asked, "What's going to happen now?"

"I imagine the sheriff will pay a visit to the Lazy R before the day is over."

"I have to get there before he does."

Alarmed, Sullivan said, "You're not going to warn them?"

"No, I won't do that, but I want to be there when the sheriff comes. I believe I can learn from Paula's response to the news whether or not she's guilty."

He tucked his blue woolen shirt into his denims and reached for his hat.

With a smile, Sullivan said, "Don't you think you should finish shaving?"

Carson glanced in the mirror, noting that one side of his face was smooth and neat but the other side still had a two days' growth of whiskers. He picked up the lather brush again. "I'm not thinking straight," he admitted sheepishly, "but my whole future is at stake. I want to do the right thing, but my heart is involved."

"The sheriff moves slowly. He'll have his breakfast, with an extra cup of coffee, before he leaves town. You should have plenty of time."

⁂

Paula was still happy over their visit to the Swedish family when she got up the next morning. And she felt even better when she later looked out the window and saw Carson tying his horse to the hitching post in front of the ranch house.

"Oh, Florence," she called excitedly, "he did come back!"

Florence rustled in from the kitchen and opened the door at Carson's knock.

"Hello, stranger," she said gaily. "We thought you'd forsaken all of us at the Lazy R."

He shook hands and came into the room where Paula waited. He took her hands and looked at her gravely. She wondered at the serious expression on his face.

"Sit down, Carson," she invited. "Will you stay for dinner? Florence is preparing a meat loaf. It's one of her best dishes."

"Thanks. I've been looking forward to another of Florence's meals."

"The food won't be ready for another hour." Direct as ever, Florence said, "Paula and I missed you when we were in Broken Bow a few days ago. Someone said you'd gone out of town."

"Yes, an emergency came up, and I had to leave town quickly. I didn't have time to send word to you."

Suddenly Eulie burst through the dining room door into the living room. His eyes were wild. And he carried a pistol in his right hand.

Florence jumped up. "Eulie Benedict! Put that gun down before you hurt somebody."

The foreman ignored her. "The sheriff and Homer Sullivan are heading this way." Turning to Carson, he said angrily, "What do you know about it?"

Paula rose to her feet. "Eulie! Carson is a guest. Don't insult him. Put that gun away."

"I don't trust him. There's something fishy going on."

A knock sounded at the door, and Eulie backed into a corner near the fireplace, the gun dangling in his hand. Carson took a stand near the dining room door. Florence went to the front door and admitted the sheriff and Homer Sullivan. Confused, Paula stood in the center of the room, looking from Carson to the sheriff to Mr. Sullivan and back to Carson.

Sullivan took a seat upon Florence's invitation. The sheriff continued to stand by the door, his hand on his holstered gun.

"Paula," Sullivan said, "we hate to barge in this way, but there's a matter concerning Gordon Randall's will that needs to be clarified. Sit down, ladies. You, too, Eulie."

"I'll stand," Eulie snarled.

⁂

Dreading this revelation, Carson watched Paula closely as Sullivan handed her a clipping from the Lincoln newspaper reporting the forged addendum to Gordon Randall's will. As she read, her face flushed before it turned ashen white. She swayed in her chair. Florence rushed to her side.

Paula's reaction suggested shock, rather than guilt, Carson decided. Leaving Paula to Florence for the moment, he turned to watch Eulie. The foreman rushed forward, snatched the paper out of Paula's lifeless hands, read the article quickly, threw it on the floor, and backed toward the outside door. The sheriff blocked his way, so Eulie turned toward the dining room where Carson stood. Taking the butt of his pistol, he broke out a window and lunged toward it, but before he escaped, the sheriff took him by the arm, pulled him back into the room, and handcuffed him. He prodded Eulie out of the room with the muzzle of his six-shooter against his back.

Carson rushed to Paula, who lay limp in the chair. Florence brought a damp cloth from the kitchen and handed it to Carson. He carefully bathed her face and hands, and as she slowly regained consciousness, her eyes shone with horror.

"I knew nothing about it," she gasped hoarsely.

"I know that," Carson assured her, but the wild expression in her eyes worried him.

"Eulie Benedict has been identified by the forger as the man who paid him a hundred dollars to draw up the counterfeit document," Sullivan said.

Paula covered her face with her hands. "I knew nothing about it," she repeated. "Please believe me."

Carson pulled her cold, trembling fingers away from her face and warmed them in his own, saying, "I do believe you."

"I believe that, too," Sullivan said. "Although when I first suspected that the addendum was a fake, I wondered if you were involved, too."

"But so we could be sure that you weren't, I didn't tell you the sheriff was coming. I wanted to see your reaction," Carson said, knowing immediately that he'd used a poor choice of words.

Paula snatched her hands from his. "You actually believed I'd be so dishonest?"

He retrieved her hands. "No, but that seemed the only way to prove it. That's why Mr. Sullivan and I went to Lincoln this week to interview the forger."

"What will happen to Eulie?" she asked.

"I don't know," Sullivan said. "The sheriff will take him to jail. He'll be charged with a crime, but I don't know if he'll be tried here or in Lincoln. He's off your hands for the time being."

Paula paced around the living room. "That settles the matter of whether I'll get the Lazy R or not. It's going to be hard to forgive Eulie for giving me false hope." She turned to Carson. "If Frank Randall isn't here by Christmas, what then? Do I just abandon the ranch since I know it can never be mine?"

"Mr. Sullivan will have to answer your legal questions, but I'd suggest that you do nothing until after the first of the year. Christmas is just a week from today, so go on with your preparations for the holiday."

The lawyer nodded agreement. "Is there someone who can take charge of the men until then?"

"Yes. Jerry Compton is the straw boss. He's capable enough for now, and he'll be a lot easier to work with than Eulie was."

After the lawyer left, Florence went to the kitchen to finish dinner preparations. Carson tenderly drew Paula into his arms. "I wish I could have spared you this embarrassment," he said.

"Strange as it might seem, I'm relieved that the ranch isn't mine, and I wish Frank Randall *would* come and claim it. Ownership of the Lazy R is more responsibility than I want. At last I forgive Dad and his nephew for causing me so much worry these past few months. I was greedy, and I feel cleansed to have that off my conscience."

"The Bible teaches that there's more to life than material possessions."

When she lifted her face, Carson briefly touched her lips

with his, and his hand caressed her hair. She knew he was right. All the possessions in the world couldn't compare to love—love for others and for that certain man in her life.

"You don't have anything to worry about now. In a few days, when you've had time to recover from this incident, we'll have that long talk," he promised. "Don't worry."

"Are you going back to Kansas for Christmas?"

"It wouldn't be practical when I intend to start the revival services a week later."

"Then, will you take Christmas dinner with Florence and me? She usually goes to her daughter's home, but she won't leave me alone this year."

"Yes, I want to be with you. I'm assisting Reverend Bailey with the Christmas Eve service. Will you be there?"

"That depends on the weather, but we're planning on it. Grace said the service will be held in midafternoon to give people time to return to their homes before dark."

"I'll count the minutes until I see you again." He kissed her cheek before he left, believing in his heart that the way was cleared for his eventual marriage to Paula.

fourteen

Her stepfather had always told Paula that the bunkhouse was off limits to her, and she had never gone inside the building. But the workers deserved an explanation of why the sheriff arrested Eulie. Winter was usually a slow time for the hands, and she knew most of them would be at home. After Carson left, she bundled into her heavy coat, threw a scarf over her head, and put on heavy boots. Her feet dragged as she left the house—this wouldn't be a pleasant task.

She knocked on the door. "It's Paula. I'd like to come in."

Jerry opened the door, and she stepped inside. In a quick glance, she saw that two of the men were playing checkers, another was reading a book, and one was repairing a bridle. The others lounged in their bunks. Heat from a potbellied stove in the center of the room made the room pleasant.

"What's going on, Miss Paula?" Jerry asked.

"The sheriff found out that Eulie had a man forge the addendum to Dad's will. He's been arrested."

All the men came to attention quickly, and she was convinced that none of them were involved in Eulie's crime.

"You don't mean it!" Jerry said.

"It's true." She took the newspaper article out of her pocket. "This is an article about the crime from a Lincoln paper. I'll leave it so you can read it. This settles once and for all that I don't have any claim to the Lazy R, but I hope you'll help me hold things together until after the first of the year. If Frank Randall doesn't show up by then, Mr. Sullivan, as administrator of the estate, will make some kind of an arrangement. Whoever takes over the ranch will need hands, so try not to worry about your jobs."

"We're sorry as can be, Miss Paula," Hal Coyner, one of the older hands, said. "Doesn't seem fair that you'll have to leave your home."

"I'm not sure I want to live here. With all these things happening, it doesn't seem like home anymore. And, Jerry, will you take over as foreman for the time being?"

"Sure I will," Jerry said. "And now that you're here, I want to talk to you about something. A man has been riding around the ranch for several weeks. We've never caught him doing anything, but we've found a lot of fresh digging. We think he's doing it."

"I saw some of those holes several days ago."

"The next time I catch him on the ranch, I'm going to bring him in. I think we have the right to know what he's doing."

"I figger he's just another galoot looking for the buried treasure," one of the checker players said as he made three jumps on the board. "King me!" he shouted to his companion.

Jerry shook his head stubbornly. "That's my opinion, too, but that don't give him any right to be diggin' holes big enough to cripple a cow or horse."

"When you see him again, bring him to the ranch house," Paula said. "I'll talk to him and tell him he's wasting his time."

So when Paula saw Jerry riding down the creek valley behind another rider the next morning, she assumed that the mysterious stranger had been trespassing again.

"Florence," she asked, "will you stay with me while I talk to the man?"

"I wouldn't miss it."

Florence settled down in a rocking chair near the fireplace and picked up a half-finished sock out of the basket beside her feet. When a knock sounded at the door, Paula opened it.

"Found him trespassing again, Miss Paula," Jerry said.

Paula moved backward a few steps. "Come in, both of you."

Jerry had a six-shooter in a hip holster, and the tense expression in his eyes indicated that he wouldn't hesitate to use it. The stranger didn't seem to be armed.

"He's been hiding a shovel and a spade in that old shack down next to the river."

Paula recognized him as the stranger Kitty had pointed out to her about the same time Carson had come to Broken Bow. She didn't ask the man to sit down. "We'd like to know who you are and why you're trespassing on Lazy R property."

The man's eyes were belligerent beneath his bushy eyebrows. He apparently hadn't shaved for several days because a stubble of whiskers covered his cheeks and chin. The man was older than Paula suspected when she'd seen him at a distance. She judged him to be in his fifties.

"Roscoe McCoy's my name. I'm from New York."

"All right. Now, why are you digging on Lazy R property?"

McCoy deliberated a few moments. Jerry fidgeted from one foot to the other, obviously wanting to force the man to talk. The consistent clack of Florence's knitting needles sounded loudly in the silence of the room.

"Can I sit down?" McCoy finally asked. "I've got a game leg."

"Of course," Paula said. "Take a chair closer to the fire."

Jerry didn't look happy at this turn of events, but Paula shook her head at him. She didn't necessarily think that she was a good judge of men, but she didn't believe McCoy was dangerous. He settled into the chair with a sigh and twiddled his thumbs for a short time.

Suddenly, seeming to have reached a decision, he pulled at a chain around his neck and brought forth a small leather bag from the front of his shirt. He extracted an envelope from the bag. "This is a letter from my grandpa, Henry McCoy, addressed to my dad." He took a piece of paper from the envelope and handed it to Paula.

She scanned the short message quickly. It was dated 1860. For the benefit of Florence and Jerry, Paula read aloud:

Dear Son:

I know you and your ma thought I was crazy to go to the goldfields, and I have missed you for the past two years. But I struck it rich. I started for home with a small party travelin' along the Oregon Trail. We've left the trail and are going north to get away from a bunch of outlaws that have been followin' us. I didn't want nobody to realize I'm carrying gold, and tonight I slipped away from the others and buried it. I ain't feelin' too good, and if I don't make it home, you can find the gold buried near a little creek a trapper told me is called the Muddy.

Paula inserted the letter back in the envelope and gave it to McCoy. She couldn't suppress a smile. "Mr. McCoy, people have been hunting that gold for years. When my dad came here years ago, he had his men fill up hundreds of holes even then. There isn't any gold on this ranch. I'm afraid you've made a long trip for nothing."

"I'd like to know why you waited so long to look for the gold," Florence said.

"We didn't get the letter for several years or more because my family moved around a lot, and it took the message a long time to catch up with us. We always wondered why Grandpa didn't come home. My dad thought it would be a wild-goose chase, and he didn't follow up on it. But I've always thought he did strike gold, and after my dad died, I didn't think it would hurt to try my luck and look for it."

"Your luck has just run out, buddy," Jerry said. "You've got to quit digging holes in our grazing land. Some of our critters are gonna end up with broken legs."

Ignoring Jerry, McCoy said, "I don't suppose you'd know where my grandpa was buried."

"I'm not sure there were any settlers in this area when that letter was written, so there wouldn't have been any cemeteries. I'm sorry," Paula said and meant it. No doubt, McCoy's grandfather was buried in an unmarked grave.

McCoy limped toward the door.

"Please stop trespassing on the Lazy R," Paula said. "If you continue, I'll have to report it to the sheriff."

"I ain't leaving town yet," McCoy said, "but I'll stay off your property." He left the house, awkwardly mounted his horse, and loped away from the ranch buildings.

Scratching his head, Jerry said, "What do you make of him? Do you reckon he's telling the truth?"

"Probably," Paula said. Glancing at Florence, she said, "What do you think?"

"Did the letter look like it was thirty years old?"

"Yes, I'd say so. It was written on the back of a store bill from a Colorado store, and the paper and writing were faded."

"Of course, he could have stolen the note," Florence said.

"If that gold ever does show up, who would it belong to?" Jerry asked.

"I don't know. Maybe it would be McCoy's," Paula said. "But he would have to prove he is related to the man who hid it. The law would probably have to decide."

"Well, I wish someone would find the stuff if it's on this spread so we wouldn't have to deal with any more would-be prospectors." Jerry put on his hat and turned toward the door.

"Florence and I are going to the Christmas Eve program in Broken Bow tomorrow afternoon. Do you men want to go?"

"All of us can't leave, but I'll go and take a few others to watch out for you. Are you going to stay overnight?"

"Not unless the weather turns bad."

੨

Reconciled to the fact that the Lazy R would soon cease to be her home, the next day Paula went early in the morning to the fenced cemetery where her mother and Gordon Randall were buried. Small cedar trees grew on the hillside, and two large cottonwood trees were inside the fence, their branches hovering over the few gravestones. In addition to the Randall graves, small stones marked the burial places of a few Lazy R cowboys. Paula knelt by her mother's headstone. Most of the snow had melted, but the ground was still frozen. She felt the cold seeping through her clothing. She knew her mother couldn't hear, but it had always helped to come here when she was troubled and pour out her hurts and frustrations.

"Mother, I'll have to leave the Lazy R, and though it's all right, I hate to leave you here. I feel very lonely today. I think you would have liked Carson. He's said a few things to make me think he will ask to marry me, but I don't know what to answer. I haven't known him very long, and I don't want him to think I'm just marrying him to get a home. Although I think I love him, I don't know if he loves me. If I marry someone around Broken Bow, I can still come back occasionally to visit you, but Carson's home is a long way from here."

When she left the cemetery, Paula didn't know if she felt better or worse. Carson really was a stranger to her, and if she married him, would she have to move to Kansas? It frightened her to even think about such a thing, for his parents might not like her at all.

fifteen

On Christmas Eve, when Paula and Florence set out for Broken Bow, Jerry and five of the other cowboys cantered behind the buckboard.

"I don't like the looks of that sky," Florence commented, tying her scarf more tightly around her head. "If it doesn't snow before morning, I'll miss my guess. I hope we're not heading into a bad winter."

"I hope not, too," Paula answered. "Mr. Sullivan will have to make some decision about operating the ranch until Frank Randall is located. Jerry isn't as competent as Eulie, but he's a good man. So I hope he can stay in charge."

Worry flitted through Paula's mind again—fears she thought she had put behind her. She *was* trusting her future to God, but she would hate to leave the Lazy R without knowing what would happen to it. When they arrived in town and entered the church, Carson greeted her at the door, and she put her concerns aside. The worship service eased her wounded spirit, as Reverend Bailey spoke on the text, "But when the fulness of time was come, God sent forth his Son."

While the burning candles brought a radiant glow into the small sanctuary, Carson assisted the pastor in dispensing the elements for communion. The peace of God filled Paula's heart when she sang with the congregation, "Joy to the world! The Lord is come!"

Dusk was fast approaching when the congregation left

the church, and a northwest wind scattered snowflakes around the town. It was a picturesque scene, but the prospect of snow urged the families who lived out of town to move rapidly toward home.

Carson walked beside Florence and Paula to their buckboard.

"You'd best ride along with us and spend the night," Florence said. "If you wait 'til morning, you might not be able to make it to the Lazy R."

Paula's heart lifted at the prospect of having Carson in their home.

"I've been invited to have supper with the Bailey family tonight, and I've accepted. But it will take a mighty big blizzard to prevent me from coming to the Lazy R. Tomorrow is an important day for me."

What does that mean? Paula mused, as she lifted the reins and the sorrels leaped forward, heading for their cozy stall in the stable. Three of the cowhands rode ahead of the vehicle, while the others rode behind them. Snow swirled around the buckboard, and with the heavy cloud cover, darkness fell rapidly. The cowboys in the lead carried lighted lanterns, and they traveled safely.

"It won't be a blizzard," Florence predicted, "but we may get a few inches of level snow."

When Paula stopped the buckboard in front of the ranch house, a horse was tied to the hitching post. Olaf Hannson huddled on the porch, but at their approach, he hurried down the steps. Taking in the situation at once, Paula and Florence climbed down from the buckboard and went to him.

"I been so vorried. The vife's time is come, and I didn't know ven you'd be home."

Florence patted his shoulder. "I'll be ready to go in a

few minutes. You go on back to your family, and I'll be there soon."

Hannson climbed clumsily on the workhorse and kicked it into action. His form soon disappeared as darkness descended on the ranch.

As she hurried up the steps, Florence called over her shoulder, "One of the men can take me in the buckboard, and I'll send the Hannson children back for you to take care of tonight."

"But when will you be back? What about Christmas dinner?"

"I'll stay as long as I'm needed. I've got most of the food prepared, so you can manage." Florence disappeared into the house, and a light soon appeared in the window.

Will my life ever be crisis free? Paula wondered. She didn't know anything about taking care of children, especially children who couldn't speak much English. She started to protest until she remembered that Christmas symbolized giving, and what better way to celebrate Christ's birth than to help others in need? *Stop thinking about your own problems and consider others!* She remembered Reverend Bailey's sermon tonight and how the angel had said that Jesus came to bring peace and goodwill to all men. Perhaps Paula Thompson was God's angel tonight to bring peace to the hearts of the Hannson children.

Olaf Hannson had looked terrified, and Florence would have her hands full with the husband and wife. Paula would do the best she could with the children to make them feel wanted.

Jerry rode up to her, leaned from his saddle, and gave the reins of his horse to one of his companions. "What's wrong, Miss Paula?"

"Florence has to go to the dugout where the Hannsons live. Do you mind taking her?"

"Not at all, but I'll switch teams. These sorrels have had enough for tonight. I'll bring the gray team." He quickly unhitched the sorrels and led them toward the stable. "I'll hurry and be ready by the time Florence is."

"She wants you to bring the Hannson children back with you to spend the night with me."

Florence had gathered a basket of supplies and was ready by the time Jerry returned with the fresh team. She hurried down the steps, and Jerry helped her into the buckboard. "Send somebody after me tomorrow afternoon," she called. Paula waved her hand that she understood, but she felt lonely and helpless.

The gray horses had been in the stable all day, and they appeared frisky. Jerry touched their flanks with the tip of his whip, and they whirled out of the ranch yard at record speed. Paula watched them out of sight before she returned to the house and started preparations for her guests.

She stirred up the coals in the kitchen stove and in the fireplace. She went upstairs and brought down the boxes of gifts for the cowboys. She set the boxes by the front door to give to Jerry when he returned. She placed the gifts she'd bought for the Hannson children under the Christmas tree—a spindly cedar on which she and Florence had tied tufts of colored fabric and draped garlands of popcorn.

She brought a pitcher of cold milk from a cabinet on the back porch, thankful that her stepfather had kept milk cows. She poured some of the milk into a pan and placed it on the back of the stove to have it ready to make hot cocoa for their evening meal. She took a box of Walter Baker & Company's chocolate from the cupboard shelf and grated enough to add to the beverage. The Hannson children would welcome it after a cold ride from the dugout.

As the stove got hotter, she stirred the corn chowder Florence had made to keep it from burning. She went upstairs and opened the grill into her dad's bedroom so heat from the downstairs fireplace would penetrate the cold room. She put fresh sheets and blankets on the bed where the children would sleep and piled several comforters on top.

Time passed quickly, but she was ready for her guests when she heard the buckboard return and Jerry halt the horses with a loud, "Whoa!"

Paula opened the door. The lanky cowboy was walking up to the door, holding on to each child's hand.

"Here you are, Miss Paula," he said jovially. "Brought you a Christmas present."

"Come in, children. I'm glad you came to keep me company."

The children reluctantly dropped Jerry's hands, but they were wide-eyed as they looked around the huge room.

"Jerry," Paula said, "will you deliver these gifts to the men in the bunkhouse? Consider them from Dad because I used Lazy R funds to buy them."

"Have you heard anything about what's going to happen to the ranch?" Jerry asked, and she knew that the futures of the ranch hands, as well as her own, were uncertain.

She shook her head. "I have no idea. I'll see Mr. Sullivan next week and find out what can legally be done. But as I told you, I'm sure you men will need to stay on, for someone will have to look after the animals. All year I've been afraid Dad's nephew *would* show up, and now I can't think of anyone I'd rather see than Frank Randall."

Jerry picked up the boxes. "Merry Christmas anyway, Miss Paula." She closed the door behind Jerry and turned to her guests. Paula told them to take off their coats, and they obviously understood some English for they removed the coats and scarves they wore.

"Come closer to the fire and tell me your names."

The boy, who appeared to be the older, said, "I'm Axel, and she's Helga."

"Where did you learn to speak English?"

"Ve live in Iowa for a year, and ve vent to school."

Helga's earnest blue eyes sought Paula's. "Vil my mother die?"

"I'm sure she won't. My friend, Florence, will take care of her. You're going to spend the night with me, and I'll take you home tomorrow. Would you like something to eat now?"

Two blond heads nodded emphatically. Axel proved to be quite a talker, and while they ate, he explained that his family had left Sweden two years ago. They had spent a year living with Britta's brother in Iowa. But Olaf wanted his own land, and he'd taken exemption rights on a piece of property near Anselmo, a town to the northwest of Broken Bow. Because of his wife's condition, they had to stop in the dugout. While they talked, Paula thought of a good solution for the Hannsons for the rest of the winter. If she was still making decisions at the Lazy R, she would move the family into the foreman's shack that Eulie had vacated. Anselmo wasn't far away, but winter was a poor time to start a new home.

She asked Helga to help wash the dishes, while Axel carried wood from the back porch and filled the wood bins. The Hannsons' clothes were filthy, so she filled a large pan with water and set it on the stove to heat. Rummaging around in Gordon's dresser, she found two of his woolen shirts, which she warmed at the fireplace.

"Take your clothes off and put these on. I'll soak the clothes, and after you're in bed, I'll rinse them and hang them behind the stove so they'll be dry by morning."

Paula poured some warm water in a big bowl and gave Helga a sponge bath. She emptied that and put clean water in the bowl and told Axel to bathe, too. She shaved lye soap into a large vat of hot water and put their clothes to soak in the soapy water.

With those chores accomplished, she took the children to the living room. She pulled the couch close to the fireplace and placed a warm blanket on it. "Sit beside me," she said. "I'll read the Christmas story from the Bible to you. After that you can finish the rest of the cocoa, and I'll take you upstairs to bed."

Helga crawled up on Paula's right, and Axel sat on her other side. They snuggled close to her, and she placed her arms around them. The children smelled of the scented soap she had used in their baths. Helga's long blond curls were still damp, but her head seemed to fit exactly into the curve of Paula's arm. For the first time, Paula sensed the stirring of maternal emotions, and she had a small inkling of what a privilege it would be to become a mother.

Paula read the biblical passages in Luke and Matthew that told of Jesus' birth.

When she finished, Axel said, "Ve always hear a story from our father on Christmas Eve." Both children turned expectant blue eyes toward her.

"I don't know many stories, but I think I can remember one that I heard last year at Christmastime."

Helga reached up and caressed Paula's face with her tiny fingers. "Tank you."

The child's touch wrapped itself around Paula like a warm blanket as she began the story:

"Martin, an old shoemaker, lived in France a long time ago. Martin had no children, and he lived alone. One Christmas Eve, Martin sat alone in his tiny shop reading the same stories I've read to you tonight. He wished he could be as fortunate as the wise men and shepherds who had seen Jesus. Then he began to wonder if Jesus were to be born in his town on this Christmas Eve, what could he give Him? He looked around his shop and saw a pair of tiny leather shoes with silver buckles. Since this was among his finest work, Martin decided that he would give those shoes to the Christ Child.

"Suddenly Martin felt a presence in the room, and he thought he heard a voice. 'Martin, you have wished that I would come to your town. Tomorrow I'm going to pass by your hut. If you invite Me in, I will be your guest.'

"Martin was so excited he couldn't sleep that night. Before daylight he got up and cleaned his shop. He covered the table with a linen cloth and put a loaf of bread, some honey, and cups on the table. He prepared a pot of tea and hung it over the fire."

The children were so quiet that Paula thought they must have gone to sleep, but when she paused, they turned to her quickly. "A good story," Axel said. "Go on."

Smiling, Paula continued, "Then the shoemaker stood at the window to watch for the Christ Child, who didn't pass by. But as he watched, he saw a street sweeper cleaning the bricks in front of his hut. The man looked half-frozen, so Martin invited him in for a cup of hot tea. The man left, and still Jesus didn't arrive.

"Soon Martin saw a young woman with a baby walking by his window. She stopped to rest in the shelter of his doorway. Her misery touched the old cobbler's heart, and he offered her shelter in his home. He gave her a slice of bread and some hot tea, and while she ate, Martin noticed that the child didn't have any shoes. He tried the leather shoes he had planned to give the Holy Babe on the child. They were a perfect fit, and he left the shoes on the child's feet. Soon the mother and child went on their way, but the Christ Child didn't appear.

"The day passed, and although Martin invited many passersby to share his hospitality, the expected Guest didn't put in an appearance. With a heavy heart, the cobbler decided that he had dreamed the voice the night before. But suddenly the room was filled with a bright light, and in his mind, all of the people Martin had helped during the day passed before him.

"The voice he had heard the night before spoke to Martin's conscience, and he listened in delight to the words of Jesus. 'Then shall the King say unto them. . . . Come ye blessed of my Father, inherit the kingdom prepared for you from the foundation of the world: For I was an hungred, and ye gave me meat: I was thirsty, and ye gave me drink: I was a stranger, and ye took me in: naked, and ye clothed me: I was sick, and ye visited me: I was in prison, and ye came unto me. . . . Inasmuch as ye have done it unto one of the least of these my brethren, ye have done it unto me.' Knowing that the Christ Child had visited him that day disguised as the people he had helped, Martin went to bed with a happy heart."

When Paula finished the story, Axel yawned and Helga

grinned sleepily. "Tank you," she whispered.

"You're welcome," Paula answered. "And now it's time for you to go to bed."

As she came downstairs after seeing that the children were comfortable and warm, Paula realized that, like Martin, she had experienced the true meaning of Christmas tonight. As she ministered to the needs of Axel and Helga, she had welcomed the Christ Child into her home and her heart.

sixteen

Despite the two inches of snow that had fallen during the night, Carson arrived by ten o'clock the next morning. When Paula went to the door to receive him, with Axel and Helga holding on to her skirts, he laughed merrily. "Well, what do we have here?" he said, kneeling on the children's level.

"Ve stayed with Miss Paula last night," Helga said.

"And did Santa Claus come to see you?"

"Ve don't know Santa Claus," Axel said. "In Sweden, an elf named *Jultomten* brings gifts."

"And he found us in Nebraska," Helga said proudly. She took Carson's hand. "Come see."

"Mrs. Hannson is ill, and Florence went to help her," Paula explained. "She sent the children to stay with me. When we take them home later on in the day, there may be another gift for Helga and Axel at the dugout." Carson smiled, indicating that he understood what the gift would be.

"Right now, there are gifts to be opened and Christmas dinner to be enjoyed. I'm not the cook that Florence is, but the children and I have managed to provide a meal."

"Smells delicious." Carson inhaled the pleasant aroma wafting from the kitchen as he took off his heavy coat. The children stood beside their small pile of gifts, expectant expressions on their faces. Smiling mischievously, he said, "We'd better eat before we open gifts."

"Nah! Nah!" Helga shouted. "Gifts first!"

"Dinner isn't ready anyway," Paula said.

Helga and Axel were fascinated with their new sweaters and the wool caps Florence had knitted for them. Helga's eyes brightened with pleasure when she unwrapped the small china doll, and Axel clutched his book in his arms.

"Dis is the first book of my own," he said.

While the children looked at their new possessions, apparently finding it hard to believe that they belonged to them, Carson murmured to Paula, "I have a gift for you, too, but I prefer to deliver it in private. Perhaps later this evening?"

"That will be fine. We should take the children back to the dugout after dinner, but it isn't a fit home for them and the new arrival. I wish they could move into a house for the winter. Eulie's shack is vacant now. It's a small sod building, but no smaller than the dugout. It would be a warm place for them, but I don't have the right to make that decision."

Thoughtfully, Carson stared into the fire. "I'm sure we can find a place for them."

For a moment, Paula was sad, knowing that tomorrow would be the anniversary of her stepfather's death, but he wouldn't have wanted her to mourn him. He had died the way he would have chosen—a quick release without pain and suffering. And her uncertain future didn't bother her as much as it had a few weeks ago. No matter what the future held for her, God was in control, just as He had been in Bethlehem many years ago. The Hannson children had been a blessing to her, and watching their happy faces as they tried on their sweaters and caps, her heart was at peace.

❧

After they finished their meal, Paula gathered everything together that she wanted to take with them to the Hannsons'. She and the children waited while Carson went to the barn and, with Jerry's help, hitched the sorrels to a wagon and drove to the house. Carson then bundled Paula and the two happy children in the wagon bed and covered them with a large buffalo-hide rug. Surrounded as they were by gifts and containers of food, Paula thought they symbolized Christmas Day at its greatest. Their bright red caps emphasized the fair skin of the Hannson children. Paula had a long blue scarf, also a gift from Florence, wound around her head.

The horses seemed eager to run, so Carson let them have their heads for a couple of miles before he slowed them to a brisk walk. He started singing, "Joy to the world! The Lord is come! Let earth receive her King."

The faces of Axel and Helga brightened, and they clapped their hands and tried to hum the tune. Paula, delight flowing from her own heart, caught a twinkle in Carson's eyes as he glanced back at her. When Carson started singing, "O come, all ye faithful, joyful and tri-umphant," Paula said, "Try to sing the words with us." The children had learned a few of the lyrics by the time they topped the hill, rode down into the small valley, and stopped in front of the dugout.

Olaf rushed to the wagon, shouting, "*God Jul*," which Paula thought meant Merry Christmas in his native tongue. Judging by the broad smile on his face, Paula knew that Britta was all right.

"Papa, Papa!" his children called as they jumped from the buckboard. "See all the presents! *Jultomten* found us in Nebraska!" Axel added.

"He found your mama, too. Come see your new baby brother."

Axel and Helga ran into the dugout, and Olaf reached up

his right hand to help Paula to the ground.

"Congratulations, Olaf!" Carson said, vigorously shaking his hand.

"We brought some of our Christmas food to share with you and also presents for you and Britta," Paula said. "Help us carry everything inside."

Florence smiled happily at them, but Paula observed that her friend's shoulders drooped and fatigue showed in her eyes. Britta lay on a pallet of quilts, holding the new baby in her arms. "Oh," Paula murmured reverently as she surveyed the crude room, the baby cradled in his mother's arms, Olaf standing beside his wife, and Axel and Helga kneeling in awe before their brother.

"It must have been like this when Jesus was born," she murmured. "I know the Bible said that He was born in a stable, but I've heard that animals were often stabled in caves in Palestine. I can imagine how the shepherds must have felt when they saw the Christ Child. What a blessing to have a baby born at the Lazy R on Christmas Day!"

"Have you picked a name for him?" Carson asked.

"Ve believe he should be named Josef, after the earthly father of our Lord."

"That's a good choice," Carson agreed.

❧

Assured that Britta was all right, Florence returned to the ranch house with Paula and Carson. She stated her intention of going to bed immediately.

"I had a rough night, so I'll probably sleep until morning. Are you going to stay tonight, Carson?"

"If I may," he said.

"The Hannson children slept in the spare bedroom last night," Paula said to Florence, "but I'll change the sheets and blankets. You get some rest."

After Florence wearily climbed the steps, Carson took Paula's hand and led her to a bench near the fireplace. He put his arm around her shoulders and pulled her close to him.

"Before I give you a gift, I want to ask you a question. It's difficult for me to believe, after knowing you for such a short time, that I've fallen in love with you, but I have. Is it too much to hope that you feel the same way about me?"

Her blue eyes meeting his dark ones, Paula said, "I'm very fond of you. I don't know if it's love."

"I want you to marry me. If you answer yes, that will be the best Christmas gift I've ever had."

Paula hesitated momentarily. If she said yes, she would be giving up the life she'd known to follow Carson where his ministry might take him. Was she ready for that? Although it hurt to think of leaving Custer County, she couldn't live in the past forever. Could she step out in faith, as many women of the Bible had done? She thought of Sarah and Rebekah, who'd followed their husbands even when it meant leaving their homes. And, of course, the Lazy R wasn't even her home now.

While Paula's spiritual nature had been undergoing a change in the past month, she had often prayed the psalmist's prayer, *"O send out thy light and thy truth: let them lead me."* She believed that God had answered her prayer by leading her to Carson, but she had to be sure. "I know so little about you. In some ways, you still seem like a stranger to me. Will you wait a few days on my answer?"

A resigned look passed through Carson's eyes. "I'd rather hoped that I could have your answer before I told you about myself. But you're right—you should know more about me before you make a commitment."

Paula wondered at the grave expression in his eyes as Carson took an envelope from his pocket.

"Merry Christmas, Paula," he said, placing the envelope in her hands. She glanced upward at him, wondering what kind of a gift would be enclosed in an envelope. Her fingers trembled, and she experienced a wide range of conflicting emotions—surprise, annoyance, anger, confusion—when she read the documents that Carson had shown to Sullivan a few weeks ago proving that he was Frank Randall, heir to the Lazy R Ranch.

Paula was slow to comprehend why he thought this was a Christmas gift for her. Trying to control the anger that she wanted to unload on him, she finally asked, "Why haven't you told me?"

"I didn't have the nerve to tell you the first day when I sensed how much you resented the nephew, whom you considered a usurper. And since my dad didn't want me to accept the ranch, I wasn't sure I'd even want to stay here. I didn't intend to deceive you, but with all the things that have happened, I couldn't find the right time to tell you. Do you forgive me?"

Stifling her conflicting emotions, Paula realized that this information had solved all of her problems. That was why Carson had considered it a gift. She knew that she should be joyful instead of angry. "I should make you suffer for all the worry you've caused me," she teased him, "but I won't. Several days ago, I had a talk with my Lord. He forgave me of my unchristian attitude about ownership of the Lazy R. Dad obviously wanted the ranch to stay in the Randall family. I'm happy he willed it to you."

"But since you're going to marry me, it will belong to *us*."

"I haven't agreed to that yet," Paula said looking at him, a curious glow in her eyes. "But I think I've discovered the reason you kept your real identity from me for so long. If I had known, you would never have been sure that I didn't marry you just to get the ranch."

He colored slightly, and Paula laughed at his discomfiture.

"It had crossed my mind," he admitted, "until I prayed about it and received the assurance that you'd be honest with me. Besides, I intend to settle in Custer County. I'm sorry to disappoint my father, but I can't take over his business. I'll continue my evangelistic work wherever the Lord calls me, but the Lazy R Ranch will be our home."

"I don't believe you should make a decision about marrying me or settling on the Lazy R until you talk it over with your parents. I can tell you have a deep respect for your father, and you won't want to hurt him. Go home and talk to him. I won't give you an answer until you come to an agreement with him. I don't want you to spend the rest of your life regretting your decision."

"I can't go until after the revival services, which start next week," Carson said thoughtfully. "And that will take us toward the last of January. You're right, though. I'll go home, but only if you go with me to meet my parents."

"Oh no!" Paula said, her pulse racing.

"You'll have to meet them sometime."

"But I'm not the woman they'd pick for your wife. I have the feeling that your parents live sophisticated lives compared to what I'm used to. I'm not sure I can fit into your life. It's probably a bad idea to even think about getting married."

Now that Paula had mentioned it, Carson figured his father would object to the marriage. Although Ira loved his wife devotedly, he didn't seem to believe that love was necessary for his son's marriage. He often suggested names of girls he thought would make suitable matches, but his father always had his eye on a girl's financial worth rather than whether Carson loved her.

"If I go, you go," Carson said stubbornly. "At first, I didn't think it was necessary, but you *should* meet my parents before you commit to marriage with me."

"But I would need different clothes—I can't go dressed like this."

She gestured to her long-sleeved blouse and black velvet, ankle-length skirt. "These are the best clothes I have, and I don't want to embarrass you before your family." Tears in her voice, Paula said, "I see now that a marriage between us won't work. Just forget it."

Not one to pay much attention to women's clothes, Carson shrugged his shoulders. "Mother buys most of her clothes in Kansas City, Missouri. It's a bigger city than where we live. She'll take you shopping for new things."

Paula shook her head.

"Mother has always fussed because she didn't have a girl to dress," he insisted. "She would like to help you buy a wardrobe."

Paula couldn't tell him that she barely had enough money to buy necessities, especially not new clothes in a big-city store, and she wouldn't accept clothes from Carson's mother. She couldn't buy a ticket to Berwyn, let alone Kansas City, and at this point, it wouldn't be right to accept any money from Carson. She just couldn't do it. She'd have to forget about marrying him.

"Is it all right to tell Florence and the cowboys that you're Frank Randall?" she asked, changing the subject.

"I don't want to keep them in suspense any longer than I have to."

"I suppose they should be told. Regardless of how my trip to Kansas turns out, I won't sell this place. It's a part of my heritage. So the men can continue to work for me just as they did for my uncle. I'll tell them tomorrow."

"And it's all right for me to tell Florence?"

"Yes, of course." He stepped close to Paula as she started upstairs. "Now that we're almost engaged, will you let me kiss you good night?"

Since she felt so strongly that she must not marry Carson, Paula hesitated momentarily. But she wanted him to kiss her, so she lifted her face. Her lips instinctively found their way to his. His caress was surprisingly gentle, and Paula felt carried away on a soft, fluffy cloud. His arms circled her waist in a tight embrace before he stepped backward.

"Good night, Paula. I pray that it's God's will for us to spend many more Christmas seasons together."

Paula felt like she was walking on air as she made her way upstairs. She sensed that his eyes followed her. At the top of the stairs, she paused, looked down at him, and threw him a kiss.

seventeen

Florence was already in the kitchen when Paula came downstairs the next morning.

"I hope you rested," Paula said. "You looked tired last night."

"I was asleep as soon as my head hit the pillow. I didn't rest a bit the night before. Britta didn't have an easy time of it, and I was worried. It's been a long time since I've delivered a baby. I'm making a big pot of venison stew for the Hannsons, and I'll take it over today. I want to see how Britta and the baby are getting along."

"How can I help?"

"Please bring some more potatoes from the storm cellar, if you don't mind."

A surprisingly warm breeze greeted Paula as she stepped out on the back porch. She took a lantern hanging from the rafters, raised the globe, and struck a match to light the oil-soaked wick. With lantern in hand, she headed across the yard to the deep cellar that served as a shelter from tornadoes, as well as a storage place for vegetables grown in the Lazy R gardens. Paula's mother had always had a big garden, and Florence had continued to raise fresh produce when she came to be Paula's companion.

She lifted the wooden door that was level with the surface of the soil and went down four steps. The dank smell reminded Paula of her childhood. Because of the many tornadoes her dad had experienced, he had learned to

133

fear them. When conditions were right for stormy weather, he kept his eyes on the southwest sky, and if there was any possibility of a tornado, he took his family to the cellar. He had provided another cellar near the bunkhouse for the cowboys to find shelter. When she was a child, Paula had often awakened in the cellar, having been carried there by her parents in response to a storm threat that had arisen in the night. So far, the Lazy R had escaped any damage from tornadoes, but the possibility was always there—a threat not to be taken lightly.

Paula filled a basket with potatoes and slowly returned to the house, noting that the warm air had melted all of the snow. It seemed like a spring day—not the last week in December. She entered the kitchen, filled a pan with water, washed the potatoes, and started preparing them. While she peeled the vegetables and cut them into small chunks, she debated how to tell Florence about Carson's identity, finally deciding that a straightforward statement was best.

"Carson told me last night that he's Dad's nephew. When his mother remarried, his stepfather adopted Carson and changed his name to Hartley. His first name is Frank— Carson is his middle name."

It took a lot to make Florence speechless. Her hands hovered over the pot of stew she was stirring, and the spoon clattered to the floor. She stared at Paula, seemingly dumbfounded for a minute.

"Why didn't he say so?" she asked indignantly. "He knew how worried you were."

"He might have if I hadn't told him about my worries the day I met him. He had considered leaving without revealing his identity until he learned about that forged document."

"Does he plan to stay here now?"

Paula knew that Florence was watching her appraisingly, but she kept peeling potatoes. "His father wants him to take over his mercantile business, so he intends to go home and talk with him. But he is keeping the ranch."

"And?" Florence prompted.

"He wants to marry me."

"Humph! And I suppose you turned him down."

"Not exactly. I want to think about it."

"And why would you do that? You've been mooning around like a sick calf ever since he's been here. Seems to me the situation couldn't be better."

"I've known him less than a month. I reckon it won't hurt to wait awhile longer."

"I suppose you're right," Florence admitted. "It might seem like you were marrying a stranger. Just don't wait too long. When the other single girls around here find out he owns this ranch, they'll swarm around him like bees around honey."

Paula didn't think she had to worry about that, but she didn't say so. If she did, Florence would only comment, "Pride goeth before destruction."

She did add, "I'm sure I wouldn't fit in with his family. His father owns a ranch in Kansas, as well as a mercantile business. I don't imagine Carson's parents will think I'm good enough for him."

Florence bristled like an angry rooster. "You're good enough for anybody, and I'd be quick to tell them so."

Paula stifled a smile. Florence didn't hesitate to criticize her, but she wouldn't allow anyone else to do so.

"We'll see," Paula said. "I'm glad the mystery of Frank Randall is finally solved and that I'm free from the management of this ranch. This past year has been one that I wouldn't want to live over." Paula then heard Carson's steps crossing the living room, and she shook her head at Florence.

He entered the kitchen, smiling, and laid his heavy coat on a chair. "Am I the only late sleeper in the house? I didn't hear you ladies get up."

"Good morning," Paula said. "We tried to be quiet so we wouldn't wake you. Florence wants to check on Mrs. Hannson today, so we're fixing some food for them."

"But I've got breakfast ready," Florence said. "You and Paula sit here at the kitchen table."

"It's nice and homey in this room," he said, looking around. "It's much more appealing than the formal meals served in the dining room at home."

Paula glanced around herself, seeing the familiar room through new eyes. Several potted plants were situated on a table near the window. Pots, pans, and baskets hung from the rafters. Bright red curtains hung at the windows, and the smell of the stew simmering in an iron kettle on the stove provided a pleasant atmosphere.

She wiped her hands on a linen towel and sat opposite him. Florence took a pan of biscuits, a plate of bacon, and a bowl of scrambled eggs from the warming oven. She poured a cup of coffee for each of them. "Eat hearty."

Paula expected Florence to make some comment about Carson's new identity, but she continued to prepare the Hannsons' food and didn't interrupt their meal.

"I'll go to the bunkhouse to talk to the men," Carson said when he rose from the table.

He made eye contact with Paula and gestured toward Florence. When Paula nodded, he said, "I'll tell them who I am and ask Jerry to give me a rundown on the work."

He shrugged into his coat, and as he moved toward the door, he said to Florence, "I don't intend to make any immediate changes at the ranch. I hope Paula will go ahead and keep the books as she did for my uncle. And that you will stay on as Paula's companion."

"I'll be here as long as Paula needs me."

"I'll go with you to the Hannsons' and stay here again tonight. What time will you be ready to go?"

Stirring the stew, Florence said, "A couple of hours, I'd judge."

"I'll check back with you." Looking at Paula, Carson said, "I'll have Jerry show me where Eulie's place is, and we'll look it over to see if it's fit for the Hannsons to live in for the winter."

Florence nodded in approval. "I've been worried about them living in that dugout. A heavy snow could collapse that timbered roof. Eulie's place is perfect for them."

❧

Carson walked toward the ranch buildings with a sense of ownership he hadn't felt before. It was a good feeling, and he was grateful that his uncle had given this ranch to him. He turned and looked back at the house. *His!* It was the first land he could call his own. And he hoped he could soon say it was his *and* Paula's.

His meeting with the cowhands pleased Carson, also, and it was a blessing to reassure these men that they could keep their jobs. They eagerly gathered around Carson and filled him in on the operation of the ranch. Jerry said that the ranch was running less than three thousand cows now— that Eulie had sold a few hundred head at the end of the summer. But it bothered him when Jerry said they didn't have all the cattle herded close to the ranch headquarters.

From experience, he knew that snowstorms could strike quickly.

When he left the bunkhouse, Carson walked up the hill to the fenced cemetery. He stood before the grave marker of Gordon Randall. It was inconceivable that this man had left his entire estate to a nephew he hadn't seen for years. "Blood must be thicker than water," he muttered. By rights, Paula should have had the ranch, but if she would marry him, it would work out to everybody's satisfaction. Surprised at the mild weather, as he walked back to the ranch buildings, he unbuttoned his coat. At the bunkhouse, he called to Jerry, "I want to get inside Eulie's shack. Do you have a key?"

Jerry and one of the other cowhands appeared at the door.

"Eulie wouldn't have trusted us with a key," the cowhand said. "You'll have to break in."

"Do you have a hatchet or crowbar handy?"

"There's a crowbar in the barn," Jerry said. "I'll pick it up and meet you at his shack. It's the one on the bank of that little draw beyond the big corral. Better take a horse. The melting snow has left a lot of mud."

Carson went inside the stable and led out a palomino, the first horse he came to. All of the Lazy R horses were excellent mounts. But if he did move to the Lazy R, he would ship his two favorite mounts from the ranch in Kansas. He rode to the shack. Jerry loped up soon after Carson arrived, dismounted, and tied his horse to the fence.

"Eulie never invited any of us into his home, so I don't know what we'll find."

Carson tried the door, found it locked, and stood back while Jerry pried it open. Enough light came through the windows to show a sparsely furnished living room, a bedroom, and a frame lean-to kitchen.

"Paula and I think we'll offer this shack to the Hannsons for the rest of the winter." Jerry looked puzzled, and Carson explained, "Those immigrants living in the dugout."

The straw boss agreed by nodding. "This is sure a lot better than where they're living now. But what'll we do with Eulie's stuff?"

"I notice he has a trunk in the bedroom. If you'll help me, we'll put as much as possible in the trunk and then find a box or crate for the other things." The two worked together and soon had Eulie's things packed away.

"Now what?" Jerry said when he stood up.

"Send somebody down with a wagon and put his things in a safe, dry place until we find out what happens to Eulie. Since he didn't get away with stealing the ranch, I imagine he'll get off easy. I just hope he leaves the country when he gets out of jail."

"I figger he will," Jerry said. "He won't be very popular in Custer County after this. About all we're doing now is putting out hay for the cattle, so I'll bring a couple of the men this afternoon to haul Eulie's stuff out of here, and we'll clean up the place." Surveying the dirt-covered floor and the ashes under the iron stove, Jerry said, "Eulie wasn't much of a housekeeper."

eighteen

Florence was ready to go to the Hannsons' when Carson returned to the house.

"Since it's such a nice day, I'm going, too," Paula said.

"Then one of you can drive the buckboard," he said, "and I'll ride the palomino. Let's leave right away. I'm a little skeptical of this warm weather. When the weather is this warm in Kansas during the winter, it's usually followed by a spell of bad weather."

"Same here," Florence said. "Weather breeders are what we call days like this."

Florence drove, and Paula sat in the bed of the buckboard and held the pot of stew to keep it from spilling. Carson cantered beside them, locating the various herds of cattle that were munching on the hay scattered over the melting snow. At least two of the herds were a long way from the ranch, difficult to look after if a blizzard should strike the area.

Smoke drifted from the stovepipe when they came in sight of the dugout.

"They're still staying warm," Florence said over her shoulder. "Olaf was fidgeting around yesterday, getting on my nerves, so I sent him to the creek after wood. He didn't get much wood, but at least he was gone for a few hours.

"Whoa!" Florence called loudly. Olaf and the two children hurried from the dugout.

"Velcome! Velcome!" Olaf called. Axel and Helga had on

the hats and gloves they'd received for Christmas.

Carson dismounted and gave Florence a hand as she climbed from the buckboard. She pulled back the leather flap and went inside. Carson tied the horses and reached for the pot of stew that was still warm. He carried it inside the dugout as Paula leaped from the wagon and followed him, the two children hanging on to her hands.

"How's Josef?"

"He's been crying!" Helga said, making a face. "I wish Jesus would come and take him back."

"You cry just like him sometimes," Axel retorted. Helga swatted him on the head with her gloved right hand.

"Children," Olaf called from inside the earthen home, "no fighting."

Paula herded the children before her into the dugout. Britta was still reclining on the pile of blankets. The room seemed damp, and Carson knew the Lazy R shack would be better for them.

While Florence checked Britta and the baby, Carson said, "Olaf, this isn't a good home for your family. We have a small place at the ranch that you can use the rest of the winter."

"No!" Olaf said, shaking his head. "Ve must go on to the homestead place."

"Your wife is in no condition to travel another fifty miles or so, and she can't stay in this dugout," Florence said sternly. "We can send for you tomorrow. She can lie down in the buckboard so the trip won't be too hard on her."

Olaf continued shaking his head, but Carson insisted. "As soon as Britta is able, we'll help you move on, but for the good of your family, you can't stay here."

Even if she couldn't speak English, Britta must have

understood the gist of their conversation, for she reached up and tugged on Olaf's coat. In a weak voice, she rattled off several sentences in Swedish.

When she finished, Olaf said, "Tank you. Ve vill move to the ranch tomorrow."

Calling good-bye to the Hannsons, Carson helped Florence and Paula into the buckboard. As they turned northward, a strong wind struck them in the face. Paula shrugged deeper into her coat and tied the scarf more securely around her neck and head. A southwest breeze had accompanied the balmy weather of the morning, but Carson felt as if the wind that buffeted them now must have originated at the North Pole.

Florence looked toward the skies. Carson was riding behind them, but he loosened the reins. His horse, probably eager to get to the stable, trotted toward the buckboard. "I don't like this sudden shift in the weather," he said.

"Neither do I," Florence said tersely. "I'd judge that the temperature has dropped ten or more degrees since we left home. And my bunion has been giving me fits all day. I'm afraid we're in for some bad weather."

A sudden blast of wind wafted snowflakes around them, and Florence urged the horses forward. "I wish we could move the Hannsons today."

By the time they reached ranch headquarters, the snowfall was heavier and the wind stronger. Jerry met them at the barn door. The snow had already started freezing, and he slipped when he approached the buckboard.

"I've sent all of the men out to herd the cattle in closer to the buildings."

"I'll go help them," Carson said. "But you'd better stay here. One of us should be near the buildings."

From the way he took charge, it was obvious to Paula that Carson was accustomed to giving orders. He'd said that he worked for his father, but she suspected that he had managed the ranch.

"I've been carrying wood to the back porch of the house and into the bunkhouse," Jerry said.

Carson nodded. "You know what has to be done."

"Be careful!" Paula called.

He waved as he urged his horse forward, and he was soon lost to her sight in the swirling snow.

❧

"You'd better drive on to the house rather than trying to walk," Jerry advised Florence. "The ground's gonna be a sheet of ice in no time. I'll ride up with you and bring the team and buckboard back. I'm glad Carson is here to take charge. I'd hate to be making all the decisions. I'll carry in some more wood while I'm up there."

"I can carry in our wood," Paula said. "You take care of things at the barn and bunkhouse."

"I'll stir up the fire in the kitchen and the living room," Florence said as they entered the house, "if you'll close all of the curtains. And it might be a good idea to hang blankets over the upstairs windows and put extra quilts on our beds."

The house was already cold. Her stepfather had put in new windows a few years earlier and had always seen to it that all of the cracks in the house were caulked tightly before each winter, but as Paula pulled the curtains, she noticed that the wind had found a few places to blow snow into the room. She took off her best coat and picked another one off the wooden rack in the living room. "I suppose Carson will be staying for a while now. If we have a blizzard, he can't get back to town for a few days."

"This is where he ought to be anyhow," Florence said. "The ranch is his, and he needs to take over. Thank God he showed up before this storm hit. I hope it won't be as bad as the one we had two years ago."

Paula remembered the blizzard of 1888 very well. The storm had come unexpectedly in the middle of January. Hundreds of people were caught away from home, but all of them had found shelter so that no lives were lost. The livestock weren't as fortunate. The cattle drifted with the wind, and hundreds perished. The Lazy R had lost about fifty head after they took shelter in a box canyon and were completely covered with snow and smothered. Some thermometers in the county registered temperatures of thirty degrees below zero. Two weeks passed before anybody from the ranch had been able to go to Broken Bow for the mail and other supplies.

As she drew the blinds and curtains, Paula worried about the Hannsons and how cold they must be. Of course, the part of the house that was dug into the side of the hill wouldn't be so bad, but the front part with only a cowhide for a door would let in snow and cold.

"God, take care of them someway," Paula prayed as she braved the cold weather to bring more logs to the back porch. She tied a rope to her waist and walked toward the woodpile, groping in the swirling snow. She tied the other end of the rope to the big block where the men sawed the wood. By the time she had brought in several wheelbarrows of wood, she couldn't see the house from the woodpile. When she returned to the kitchen, she hovered close to the stove and stretched out her cold hands to the heat. "What can I do now?" she asked Florence.

"Get warm, and then you can stir up a batch of biscuits. I'm trying to make extra for the cowhands. They're going to be too busy to cook."

Keeping busy in the kitchen helped pass the time for Paula. She kept glancing at the clock, wondering about Carson and the cowboys. Sometimes the wind howled around the ranch house with such ferocity and volume that she wanted to scream.

When Florence assured her that there was nothing more she could do, she went into the living room and drew a chair close to the fire where it was cozy. It was several degrees colder when she walked a few feet from the fireplace. She moved chairs close to the fire for Florence and Carson, too, knowing that some of them would be up all night to keep the fires burning.

By four o'clock it was already dark, and Paula lit the lamps in the living room before she went into the kitchen. She hurried through the frigid dining room, being careful to close the doors behind her. Florence had prepared a large skillet of hash, a pot of white beans, and two pans of corn bread. She was now frying doughnuts.

The room was warm, and the windows were steamed over. Paula used a cloth to wipe off the window that looked toward the outbuildings, but she saw only a white world. Hearing steps on the back porch, she hurried to open the door. Carson, Jerry, and Hal Coyner were removing ropes from their waists. They shook snow from their clothes before they walked inside.

"We can't do anything more tonight," Carson said. He took off his hat and gloves and held his hands to the warmth of the fire. "It was too dangerous for us to be out any longer—not only danger from the frigid temperatures but also because it's too easy to get lost. I've given orders for anyone who has to go outside tonight to travel in pairs."

"Jerry, I'm glad you brought someone with you," Florence said. "We've fixed your suppers. Can you carry a pot of beans, some corn bread, biscuits, and doughnuts back to the bunkhouse?"

Jerry laughed. "We'll manage! That food will taste good."

"I can carry the pot of beans," Hal said. "You can put the other things in a basket."

"Don't take any chances tonight," Carson warned them. "Cattle can be replaced. Men can't."

After they'd eaten their supper, Carson said, "I'm not going to bed. I'll keep the fires going in both rooms. If the wind should blow down the chimneys, we could have a fire we don't want."

"But I can spell you," Florence protested. "You should get some sleep."

"I'll sleep tomorrow," Carson said. "I won't rest if I get into bed, so don't worry about me."

Paula hurried upstairs after a good-night kiss from Carson. She stayed warm in bed, but the strong wind whistling around the eaves kept her wakeful most of the night.

nineteen

When Florence and Paula came downstairs the next morning, Carson was in the kitchen looking out the window. Heavy snow was still falling, and there were drifts, five or six feet deep, between the barn and the house. In a few places, the ground had been swept clear of snow by the spinning wind.

Carson yawned, and Paula noticed the lines of fatigue around his face. Although she had been physically drawn to him before, she was observing Carson in a crisis now, and she liked what she saw. She knew he had the qualities of manhood, leadership, and compassion that would make any woman proud to be his wife.

He greeted her with a smile. "Did you rest any?"

"I couldn't sleep," Paula said. "I kept thinking about the Hannsons."

"I can't risk the lives of the men to go after them until the snow stops, but we'll make an effort to rescue them as soon as we can."

"How cold is it?" Paula asked, as Florence put on her big flour-sack apron and started to work.

"When I brought in the wood a little while ago, I checked the thermometer. It was ten below."

"It's not snowing as hard as it was last night at dark, so maybe it'll let up soon. After I fix some breakfast, you ought to take a nap," Florence said.

"I'm ready to eat, but I won't sleep. I napped a few times

147

last night. I'll be all right."

By noon, the snow had lessened to flurries, and Carson told them that he could make it to the bunkhouse.

"You shouldn't go alone—I'll come with you," Paula said.

He put his arm around her waist and pulled her close. "Look the other way, Florence," he said lightly.

A satisfied *humph* greeted his remark, as Carson bent toward Paula and kissed her nose then her lips. "I always enjoy having you with me," he said, "but I want you to stay in the house now. I'll take a shovel with me if I do run into any drifts, but as far as I can see, I won't have too much trouble reaching the bunkhouse. It isn't the amount of snow but the extreme cold that's the greatest danger. The men will be watching. I'm going after the Hannsons if it's possible. Jerry knows this country better than I do, so I'll take his advice about it."

Paula wanted desperately to go with them, not only because she was concerned about the Hannsons, but also because she would worry about Carson. But she did as he asked—his job would be easier if he didn't have to worry about her. "Let us know what you decide," she said.

Paula watched Carson's progress from the window. He made a few detours around snowdrifts, and in one spot, it was easier to tunnel through the snow than to go around it. It took him more than a half hour to reach the bunkhouse. Sending up a prayer for Carson's safety, she finally turned to help Florence.

≈

Carson opened the bunkhouse door, and the puff of warm air felt good to his numb face and fingers. Several of the cowhands stood around the stove. "Everything all right at the house?" Jerry asked.

"Yes. What about here?"

"We've been to the barn and stables—all the stock are good there—but the horses and the cattle in the corrals are huddled together between drifted spots. I'm afraid some of them will smother to death. We're going to shovel enough snow to give them room to walk around."

"I'm concerned about the loss of cattle and horses, but human life is more important. Do you think it's possible for us to get to the dugout where that Swede family is staying?"

Jerry's face blanched at the thought. "I don't know, but I reckon we've got to try. They might have perished already, and then we'd be risking our lives for nothing."

"I won't order any of you to go," Carson said, "but I'm going to try to reach them."

All of the men volunteered to help, and Carson thanked them, saying, "Most of you are needed here."

"I'll go with you," Hal said. "We can use the sled we use to haul hay to the cattle when there's snow on the ground. There will be room to bundle all of them onto one sled."

Hal was a grizzled, stooped man who must have weathered many blizzards. Carson thought he could be depended upon to make the rescue if anyone could.

"I'll go, too," Jerry said. "Ought we to start a fire in Eulie's shack?"

"I wouldn't. They can stay at the house tonight. Let the men go ahead and see to the livestock."

"We rigged up a snowplow a few years ago," Jerry said. "We put a couple of plow blades on the front of a big sled. I'll drive that to break a road. The sooner we start, the better."

"I'm ready. The few miles to the Hannsons' will seem a

lot longer today." Carson didn't go back to the house, for he was sure Paula would watch what they were doing. He hitched a team of draft horses to the sled while Jerry and Hal rigged up the snowplow and harnessed two mules to it. The other men were scattering hay on top of the snow in the corrals and shoveling snow over the fence, trying to make room for the cattle to move around and feed.

They loaded some shovels, spades, and ropes on the sled. Hal picked up the reins, and Carson settled on the floor beside him. Jerry led the way out of the barnyard, and the plow made a decent pathway for Hal and Carson to follow, although it probably wouldn't be so easy when they got into open country. Florence and Paula came out on the front porch and waved to them. He knew that both of them would be praying for a safe outcome of their journey.

Surveying the sky, Carson said, "The clouds seem to have lightened up so maybe the snow is over."

In his gruff voice, Hal said, "That's the way I figger. It's the cold weather that's gonna be bad now. It may drop lower tonight than last night. When it's that cold, it's harder on the cattle than the snow."

"I hate for animals to suffer, but right now, we have human lives to consider. I pray that we can get the Hannsons out of that dugout and to the Lazy R today. They couldn't survive extreme temperatures very long."

" 'Course being underground gives them some protection." Hal paused and looked around. "We're movin' along at a good pace. Jerry's doin' a good job findin' the best way to get through the snow. We'll probably be there in an hour. And it'll be quicker headin' back."

Carson knew it was a lack of faith, but he dreaded what they were going to find when they reached the dugout.

When they finally topped a knoll and looked down on the Hannsons' temporary home, he stared in amazement and concern. He had hoped to see smoke coming out of the pipe, but the whole front of the dugout had collapsed, taking the stovepipe with it.

Hal pulled his sled beside Jerry's rig. "Don't look good, does it?" Jerry said.

Sick at heart, Carson shook his head. "The snow was too heavy to support that sod and timber roof. I should have made them move yesterday. Let's hurry down there. If any of them are alive, we'll have to reach them as soon as we can."

The two vehicles slipped and slid down the small incline as the two drivers urged the teams to greater speed. As soon as Hal stopped the sled, Carson jumped to the ground and picked up a shovel. He tried to see over the pile of snow and sod that blocked the entrance, but he wasn't tall enough.

"Olaf! Olaf! Can you hear me?"

"Ve are here," Olaf said weakly.

Carson spread out his hands and looked upward. "Thank You, Father. Thank You." He then called to Olaf, "Are you all right?"

"I tink so," Olaf answered, "but ve have snow on us."

"There are three of us, and we can soon dig you out. We have a sled to take you to the Lazy R."

The snow mixed with the sod was heavy, and Carson soon pulled off his coat and laid it on the sled. After they had tied their teams, the two cowboys joined him. Sweat poured from Carson's body as if he were taking a steam bath before they finally got enough snow moved so he could climb over the fallen roof timbers and peer into the dark dugout. "I'm here now, Olaf."

The Hannsons were all huddled together, wrapped in comforters and blankets that were covered with a skim of snow. Olaf lifted a comforter from his face, and the heads of the two children popped out of the heap of blankets and quilts. "Ve covered from head to foot and de good God has kept us warm."

"The covers, they are heavy," Axel said, "and Helga has been kicking me."

Carson laughed in relief that they seemed to be unharmed. "What about Britta and the baby?"

"Not so goot—but Britta's milk has kept the baby alive. Ve could reach some of our food, and ve ate snow for our thirst."

"We'll dig you out as soon as we can." Carson jumped off the pile of snow and picked up the shovel again.

"This is hard digging," Jerry said, "and we'll get too hot if we keep at it this steady. We'll need to rest once in a while."

"A good suggestion. My shoulders are already feeling the strain from the little shoveling we've already done. Two of us can work while the other one takes a break. You and I can pull the first shift while Hal takes a breather. We won't have to move all of the snow—just enough to clear a tunnel wide enough to bring the family out."

"Do they have any livestock?" Hal asked.

"Two horses," Carson said.

"I'll look around and see if I can find any sign of them while you two dig."

Carson and Jerry had removed about three feet of the debris when Hal came running toward them. "I've found that team," he said, gasping to catch his breath. "They're huddled together beside the Hannsons' wagon, but they're almost covered with snow—just their heads and shoulders sticking out. If we don't dig them out, they can't last much longer."

Carson felt pressured to rescue the Hannsons and take them to the ranch, but he couldn't bear to have animals suffer either. It was a hard decision, but he said, "Jerry, go help him dig the team out, and I'll carry on here. Olaf can't afford to lose his horses."

As Carson got closer to the inside of the dugout, the shoveling seemed easier, and he decided that he had shoveled through most of the roof timbers. He was only a few feet from the Hannsons, when he put his shovel under a portion of snow that he couldn't lift. He kicked at the lump with his foot, trying to break it into smaller pieces.

He stopped suddenly and stared at a leather bag lying at his feet. He kicked it again, but it didn't budge. Bending over, he wiped away ice and snow until he could read the printing on the bag: COLORADO SPRINGS, 1860. He dropped the shovel and picked up the bag with both hands. Even at that, he could hardly lift it.

He had found the lost treasure! It had apparently been in the roof of the dugout all these years. Coming to a quick decision, he dug a hole in the pile of debris they had tossed aside. He dragged the bag inside the hole and threw snow and sod over it. He couldn't let anyone know about his discovery until he decided what to do with it. If the gold belonged to Roscoe McCoy, he could have it, but now was no time to make quick decisions. After they moved the Hannsons to safety, he'd deal with the treasure. The bag was completely hidden by the time the two cowboys returned.

"We got the snow off them," Jerry said, "but they're shivering and in bad shape. I don't figger they'll live."

"They're too weak to take to the ranch," Hal agreed.

"When we have the Hannsons safe, we can take the two horses into the dugout. We'll bring hay and grain for them tomorrow."

After the Hannsons were loaded on the wagon, Jerry took some of the blankets they had brought from the Lazy R, wrapped them over the backs of the trembling horses, and led them into the dugout.

Following the trail they had cleared earlier through the snowdrifts, Carson started toward ranch headquarters with the Hannsons, leaving Hal and Jerry to make the two horses as comfortable as possible until the next day. A herd of antelope raced across the trail in front of them, trying to escape two coyotes that struggled through the deep drifts in an effort to catch their prey.

"The coyotes barked around the dugout all night," Olaf said. "Ve feared they vould come inside. I vas vakeful, ready to drive them away if they tried to harm us."

"These blizzards are hard on the wildlife, too," Carson said. "They struggle to survive just as humans do."

Axel had begged to sit on the seat with Carson, and his father had agreed. The boy was covered in warm clothes except for his eyes, which were animated at the adventure. Carson was sure that this was one childhood experience Axel would never forget. Although he was no longer a child, Carson wouldn't forget it either—especially the discovery of the bag of gold that people had searched for through the years.

The baby cried weakly from time to time, and Carson prayed the child would survive this ordeal. Keeping a watchful eye on the family behind him, he drove carefully toward the ranch, but his mind was active, trying to decide the right way to deal with his discovery.

Carson bypassed the ranch buildings and drove to the house. Some of the men had shoveled a path to the front porch, and when he halted the team, Florence and Paula hurried out to greet them.

"Are they all right?" Paula called anxiously, as Carson jumped to the ground.

"Yes. The roof of the dugout caved in, but the section inside the bank provided shelter for them."

"We've put a bed in the living room for Olaf and Britta," Florence said. "I want to keep an eye on her for a few days before they move to their home."

Carson rounded the side of the sled, took Axel's hand, and helped him to the ground. The boy raced around the yard, laughing and jumping into snowdrifts. Carson reached under the covers and lifted Britta into his arms. When Olaf protested that he could carry his wife, Carson said, "You bring Josef."

Helga wiggled out of the heavy covers and jumped off the sled, immediately needing to dodge a snowball Axel threw at her. Olaf yelled at the children, and they followed the others into the house.

When Carson laid Britta on the bed, Florence said, "The rest of you go to the kitchen and get some warm food. I'll take care of Britta and the baby." She waved her hand imperiously. "Scoot now. I'll manage things in here."

"I'll take the sled and team to the barn," Carson said. "Be back soon."

Carson had stabled the team, given them a rubdown, and provided them with grain and water by the time Hal and Jerry drove into the barnyard. Two of the ranch hands came from the bunkhouse.

"The rest of the men are out on the range, checking on the cattle and horses," one of them said. "We thought some of us ought to stay here with Florence and Miss Paula."

"That's good thinking. Any livestock losses?" Carson asked.

"We met two of the men on our way back," Jerry said. "They've found a few dead cattle—mostly old cows—but it looks like we've escaped without any major losses."

"Be sure that all the men are in for the night, and then all of you rest. It's getting colder by the minute, and I want all of you inside. Thanks for helping with the Hannsons."

As he walked toward the house, Carson heard Hal say in his deep voice, "Boys, we've got a good boss. He knows how to give orders, but he sure does pitch in and do his share of the work."

"Yeah! It's gonna be like havin' Gordon Randall around again," Jerry agreed.

Even without hearing the cowboys' opinion, the past two days had convinced Carson that his place was at the Lazy R. He only hoped his father would agree with him.

With the Hannsons sleeping in the living room, Axel in Carson's bed, and Helga bunking with Paula, there was little opportunity for privacy in the ranch house. But noting the look of longing in Paula's eyes, Carson realized that she wanted some time alone with him as much as he wanted her to himself for a few minutes.

When Florence took the children upstairs to put them into bed, Carson said, "Paula and I will wash the dishes and clean up the kitchen. I'm going to stay up all night anyway to keep the fires going."

Perhaps sensitive to their need to be alone, Florence agreed.

When Florence left the kitchen, Carson grinned at Paula. "That was a flimsy excuse to have you to myself for an hour or so, but I wanted to talk to you."

"I'm not complaining," she said, a timid smile lifting the corners of her mouth.

Since their return, everyone had vied for the opportunity to tell about their experiences during the blizzard and the rescue mission, so there wasn't much left to be said about that. They chatted aimlessly while Paula washed the dishes and Carson dried them and put them on the table ready for the next morning. Paula filled the teakettle and a large kettle with water and placed them on the back of the stove.

Carson carried in enough wood to keep the fires going through the night. Paula was sitting on a chair near the stove when he finished. He lifted the round lid of the stove and placed more wood on the hot coals. He settled into the chair next to Paula and moved as close to her as possible. "I've made up my mind to live here and take over management of the ranch. I hope that by now you'll agree to live here as my wife. We haven't known one another very long, but considering all the events we've shared, I feel like I've known you for a much longer time. There isn't any doubt that I love you, and I believe God chose to bring us together."

"I still have reservations about how your parents will accept me, but all day, when I knew you were risking your life to help the Hannsons, I realized how much you mean to me. I want to marry you, and since this fulfills all of my dreams—to have a man I can love and still live in this place that has been home to me—I don't know why I hesitated when you asked me a few days ago. Yes, Carson, I will marry you."

As Carson hugged his fiancée tightly, Paula snuggled close to him. "I feel so secure in your arms."

Carson allowed himself to enjoy the moment before finally saying, "We'll still make arrangements for you to meet my parents, but I know that Mother will love you as much as I do. Father? I'm not really sure, but he'll have to accept my choice of a wife just as he must accept that I'm going to make my home at the Lazy R." Carson paused as he thoughtfully considered his words. "I was born here, and please God, I'll live here until I die. Now I have something else to tell you that may cause more trouble. I found the hidden treasure."

The disbelieving expression on her face amused him, so he quickly related how he had uncovered the bag of gold. "I don't know what to do with it. Do you have any ideas?"

She shook her head slowly.

"Just because it was found on the Lazy R doesn't give me any claim to it. But what if it doesn't belong to Roscoe McCoy either? I'd like to get it into the hands of the rightful owners, but I'm not inclined to spend a lot of money searching for them. It could take years to do that," Carson said.

"My first idea is that we must *not* let the general public know about it. Maybe we should confide in the sheriff and Mr. Sullivan and ask for their advice. Dad trusted both of them."

"I can't think of any better plan," he agreed.

twenty

A week later, the Hannsons had been moved into their temporary home, and the cowboys had rounded up all the livestock that had strayed during the storm. Carson considered that they were fortunate to lose only twenty head of cattle and two horses. Reports received by word of mouth through cowhands from other ranches indicated the Lazy R had weathered the storm better than most ranchers. The sheriff and two other men from Broken Bow traveled on snowshoes throughout the county to ascertain if anyone needed help. The sheriff brought a message from Reverend Bailey that he had postponed the revival.

As soon as the snow had hardened so the trail to Broken Bow was passable, Carson and Paula started to town, planning to stay overnight to give them enough time to decide what to do with the gold nuggets. When they were out of sight of the ranch buildings, Carson swung the sled southward, avoiding drifts, until he reached the road they had cleared on their way to rescue the Hannsons.

Paula wore her heavy cape, and she had a blanket wrapped over her lap and around her legs. Florence had dropped three hot bricks into a gunnysack and insisted they put them beside their feet. Carson was sure the bricks would be cold before their warmth could penetrate their heavy boots, but he hadn't argued. Nothing could dim his pleasure in this trip. Paula in a blue woolen bonnet and a matching muff—the color of which was the same as her eyes—was a sight to set his pulses racing.

"What if the gold is gone?" she asked as they approached the dugout.

"Then I've had a bad dream and will be relieved to find there isn't any gold."

"Someone could have found it and taken it away."

"Not likely that anyone has been digging in the debris of that old dugout in subzero temperatures. As soon as the weather warms up, I'm going to have the cowboys destroy the dugout. I don't want anyone else moving in there."

Paula stayed in the buckboard while Carson took a spade and shovel from the back of the buckboard to uncover the leather bag. He hadn't had time to bury it deeply before he'd heard Hal and Jerry coming, so he soon found what he was looking for. The thought crossed his mind that there may have been more treasure than he had discovered, but he didn't search any further. If anyone found more treasure, they were welcome to it.

With an effort, he lifted the gold into the buckboard, covered it with a saddle blanket, and set out for town. He wasn't comfortable hauling gold nuggets, which would be worth more now than when the ore had been dug years ago. But the sun was shining, the wind was blowing from the south, and he had a beautiful woman beside him. He enjoyed the drive.

"If we'd known the weather was going to turn out this well, Reverend Bailey probably wouldn't have postponed the revival," Paula commented.

"Yes, but he didn't know that when he sent me the message. Besides, I imagine a lot of ranchers are still snowed in. Even if they aren't, they're probably busy trying to keep their cattle alive during the cold weather. We'll have more success later on. Now that I'm going to be living here permanently, we can set a date to suit everybody." The postponement was a relief to Carson. With the traumatic events during the month of December, he hadn't had the right emotional or spiritual attitude to prepare sermons.

"And you did write to your parents?"

Carson tapped his left coat pocket. "I have it right here, and it will be on the evening train going south. I told them of our plans and asked their blessing. I hope we get it."

"I hope so, too," Paula said.

Carson didn't stop at the post office, for he was eager to do something with the precious bag he was hauling. Stopping in front of Sullivan's office, he tied the horses to the hitching post. He helped Paula to the ground and looked up and down the street. No one was in sight, so he lifted the leather bag out of the wagon. Paula hurried up the steps to open the door.

Sullivan was alone, and he curiously appraised the load Carson carried. He motioned them into his office. After answering the lawyer's questions about how the Lazy R fared in the blizzard, Carson said, "I found the lost treasure."

The lawyer's first reaction was surprise, but he soon burst into laughter. "Son, you've been here about six weeks, and you've sure caused our citizens to sit up and take notice. What *are* you going to do next?"

With a fond glance at Paula, Carson said, "Get married and settle down on the Lazy R."

"That's just what I hoped you would do. But about the gold—I wish you'd never found it. If the news gets around, people will be coming out of the woodwork to claim it. I don't know what to do with it."

"Neither do I," Carson admitted. "But the bag is old

and came from Colorado, so it does fit in with the tales told about the prospector. I've been thinking about it for a week. It's still in chunks of ore, but there are enough gold flecks in it to cause anyone to think it is gold."

"But there's such a thing as fool's gold—pyrite—that a lot of miners mistake for gold," Sullivan replied.

"Could we send samples of this ore to an assayer and find its worth before we make any decisions? It might not be worth bothering with."

"We can send some samples to an assayer in Denver on the railroad's express car. I've got room in my safe to lock up the rest of the ore until we know how rich a strike the prospector made."

Carson nodded. "The sooner we do that, the better. Is Roscoe McCoy still in town?"

"Yes. He'd given up and was going to leave, but the blizzard closed the railroad tracks. I wouldn't say anything to him about what you've discovered. If the prospector really found gold, we can't turn it over to McCoy until we're sure he should have it. The man who left this bag might have a lot of relatives who should inherit." Sullivan shook his head. "I still wish you hadn't found the treasure."

"Believe me, I wasn't looking for it!" Carson opened the bag, and Sullivan lifted several pieces of the ore and inspected it carefully. Some of the samples were quite golden, while others held only a few flakes of gold.

"It could be gold," the lawyer said, "but the only way anyone can tell pyrite from gold ore is by heating it. Real gold won't react when it's hot, but pyrite smokes and sends out a bad odor. I once saw a piece of real gold before it was processed, but I don't have any idea what this is."

"I'm willing to send the samples to Denver, but I want to

keep quiet about my discovery until we get the report."

Sullivan chose a few samples, wrapped them in heavy paper, and tied the bundle securely. He stored the rest in his safe, whirled the knob, and gave Carson a receipt. He took his coat off the rack by the door. "We have fifteen minutes to catch that train."

"I'll stop by the hotel while you do that," Paula said to Carson, "and arrange for our rooms. You can let me know when you want to eat supper."

Carson and Sullivan headed toward the depot after they left Paula at the hotel. By the time they made arrangements for the shipment, they heard the train approaching in the distance and sat on a bench beside the depot to wait. With smoke pouring from its stacks and the whistle blowing, the train came to a screeching halt.

When the express car stopped several yards from the depot, Sullivan said, "You might know the express car would be the last one."

Carson and Sullivan headed toward the guarded car with the stationmaster to be sure the package was shipped. When they passed a passenger car, Carson stopped dead in his tracks and grabbed Sullivan's arm. His parents were descending the train's steps!

Mary Hartley was a slender woman, above average height, and she walked with dignity and grace. Carson had inherited his dark features from her. Ira was an inch or two shorter than his wife, and a closely cropped, reddish beard covered the lower half of his face. His dark blue eyes critically surveyed the small town.

Carson stood speechless while his mother approached him, a smile on her face. "How did you find out we were coming and arrange to meet us?" she asked.

"I *didn't* know," he stammered.

She kissed his check. "Aren't you happy to see us, Carson?"

"Why. . .of course! But it is a surprise."

Ira stepped forward and shook hands with Carson. "We *wanted* to surprise you. We haven't heard anything from you since you left home, and we thought we'd better find out what was going on."

"We'd like to find a hotel as soon as possible," his mother said. "A blizzard delayed us for two days, and we're very tired."

Carson became aware that Sullivan was still standing beside him. He introduced the lawyer to his parents. With a significant look, he said, "Mr. Sullivan, will you tend to that matter while I show my parents to a hotel?"

When Sullivan walked away, Ira demanded, "What matter? What have you gotten yourself into?"

Now that he was recovering from the shock of his parents' arrival, Carson realized that they had come at an opportune time. Paula and his parents could meet without her making the trip to Kansas City, and he wouldn't have to leave Nebraska.

"It will take a long time to tell you all that's happened since I arrived in Broken Bow. Let me arrange for your luggage to be delivered to the Inman Hotel. I'll help you get settled, and we can talk later. I'll tell you this much—I've lived a lifetime since I came to Broken Bow."

Accustomed to the larger hotels, Ira wasn't pleased to learn that they wouldn't have the comfort of a suite of rooms. His wife wasn't as hard to please. "All I want is a bed and some warm water for a bath. We'll take whatever you have," she said to the clerk. Most of the time, his mother was docile and didn't cross her husband, but when she did set her foot down, Ira didn't argue with her.

Ira registered and received a key to Room 208. The clerk then turned to Carson. "Here's the key to your room." He looked at the register. "Are these your parents?" he asked, a pleased expression on his face. "I couldn't put them near your room because I've already put Miss. . ."

Carson snatched the key out of his hand. "I'm sure they will be pleased with the room you've given them," he said. He intended to tell his parents about Paula as soon as possible, but he didn't want them to hear it in the hotel lobby.

He walked up the steps behind his parents. "Supper is served in the dining room at six o'clock. The food is very good. Will that give you enough time to rest?"

"Yes," Mary answered. "I want a bath more than anything else. We were stranded between towns for twenty-four hours, and although we had food, we didn't have water for washing. We'll be ready at six."

When his parents had entered their room, Carson hurried down the hall. Dinner at six o'clock would give him three hours to convince Paula that she had nothing to fear from his parents. And he thought it would take that long. He knocked on her door. When she answered, he identified himself.

She opened the door, and perhaps sensing his excitement and surprise, she asked, "Is something wrong?"

"No, actually I believe that everything is perfect." He told her about his parents' arrival. "You won't have to go to Kansas. They're only a few doors down the hall, so you can meet them tonight."

After Carson convinced Paula that his parents were eager to see her and that her clothes would be perfectly all right, he left her to get ready while he went to his own room.

৯৯

Agitated, Paula paced the floor of her room. She was terrified to meet Carson's parents. It wouldn't be so bad if she had some new clothes, but she had no choice except to wear the dark blue wool dress that Florence had made for her a year ago. When Carson came to escort her to dinner, he insisted that she was beautiful and that he thought her dress was appropriate.

She walked down the hall at his side, feeling much like a prisoner must feel on the way to be executed. Carson knocked on the door of Room 208. Paula clutched his arm, and her pulse began to beat erratically.

"Come in," Mary invited.

Carson opened the door and stood back to let Paula enter the room first. His mother was sitting on the side of the bed, and she turned startled eyes from Carson to Paula. Ira had been standing in front of the dresser and watched their entry through the mirror. He whirled quickly.

"Father, Mother, I want you to meet Paula Thompson. She is Uncle Gordon's stepdaughter. Her mother married him when Paula was a child. She's lived at the Lazy R since then. Her mother died a few years before Uncle Gordon."

Mary stood and crossed the room to shake hands with Paula. "I'm glad to meet you," Mary said. "I didn't know my brother-in-law had married."

Paula didn't know what to say. She was relieved when Carson continued, "Paula and I are in love, and we plan to be married soon. It's good that you've come to Broken Bow, and I hope you'll stay for the wedding."

To give her future in-laws credit, although Mary's face blanched and Ira's turned red, they didn't try to dissuade them. Mary kissed Paula's cheek and embraced her son. After clearing his throat a time or two, Ira said, "Then I wish you both much happiness."

Paula knew Carson was still concerned that his father would try to persuade him to return with them and take over the running of the mercantile business. She was still a little surprised when he tackled that subject immediately. "And we intend to establish our home on the Lazy R. I'm taking over management of the ranch."

"But what about the future you could have in the business world of Kansas City?" Ira argued. "The town is growing, and you can grow with it. I'm getting older. I need you beside me. Besides, your mother will miss you if you move to the Lazy R."

Paula watched nervously as Carson looked at his mother, who smiled at him and moved to her husband's side. "Ira, you have many years yet. And we won't lose Carson. I'm sure he'll visit us often."

Ira Hartley dropped heavily into the rocker beside the window. Carson walked to his side, knelt by the chair, and put his arm around his father's shoulders. "I'm sorry, Father. I'm a rancher, and you can't make anything else out of me."

After a few agonizing sighs, Ira lifted his head and shook Carson's hand. "I know, son. I won't stand in your way any longer."

Paula quietly sighed with relief as Carson exchanged an exultant look with her. The way was open for them to have a happy marriage with his parents' blessing.

epilogue

Paula sat on a stool in her bedroom while Kitty and Grace fluttered around her, determined that not a hair would be out of place nor a wrinkle of any kind be seen in her wedding gown as she walked down the stairs to become Mrs. Carson Hartley.

Her sudden marriage seemed almost like a dream. Three months ago, she hadn't known there was such a person in the world as Carson Hartley. In about fifteen minutes, she would become his wife.

After Carson's parents gave their approval of the marriage, they set the wedding date for Valentine's Day. The Hartleys had stayed in Broken Bow, rather than return home. After spending a few days looking over the Lazy R, Ira Hartley had even admitted that his son had made a good decision in staying with the ranch.

Everyone agreed that Carson and Paula should get married at the ranch—the place where Carson had been born and the place Paula had called home for most of her life. Now it would be the place they'd both call home and, if God so blessed, raise children of their own.

While Grace brushed her hair and fashioned it into a large coil on top of her head, Paula's mind wandered over the events of the past two and a half months. Since it had been in Lincoln that Eulie Benedict had arranged for the forged addendum to Gordon Randall's will, he had been transferred to Lancaster County to stand trial for his crime.

The assay report from Denver had proven that the bag of ore was pyrite instead of gold and of little value. Roscoe McCoy left town without knowing that Carson had found the ore. He had left his address, and Carson sent him a copy of the report. He also asked a county newspaper to write an article about his discovery to keep others from digging on the Lazy R, hoping that the myth of the lost treasure was laid to rest.

Paula's mind stopped wandering when Kitty said, "It's time for you to get dressed."

Carson's mother had ordered the wedding dress from Kansas City, and Paula felt like a queen when Kitty dropped the white silk dress over her head. The gown was decorated with lace and bands of satin ribbon on the bodice, and it was edged with opalescent beads. After Kitty fastened the tiny pearl buttons down the back of the dress, Grace fitted a floor-length, white lace veil over Paula's hair.

"Stand up and look at yourself," Grace murmured. "You're beautiful!"

The woman who stared back from the mirror *was* beautiful, but Paula didn't think the image looked like her. She hoped Carson would like the way she looked now. When Grace opened the door, Paula heard the murmur of excited voices in the living room. As she glided down the stairs, the presence of her mother and Gordon Randall seemed to hover over her. How pleased they would have been to know that Carson and she would be starting their wedded life at the Lazy R.

Florence, the Hannson family, and all of the Lazy R hands had crowded into the room, and they stood when Paula reached the foot of the stairs. A hush fell over the group as Paula and Grace made their way to the front of the fireplace where Carson and his father waited for them. Reverend Bailey opened his Bible and began the time-honored ceremony.

"Dearly beloved, we are gathered here. . . ."

Paula's heart danced with excitement when she felt Carson's gaze upon her. His eyes brimmed with tenderness, and she remembered what he had said the night before: "My love for you almost equals my love for God. As God loves us with an everlasting love, so do I love you. I will love you and cherish you all the days of my life."

Even as they repeated the vows Reverend Bailey read to them, Paula knew that the promises they had made to each other the night before were the commitments they would cherish for the rest of their lives.

A Letter To Our Readers

Dear Reader:

In order that we might better contribute to your reading enjoyment, we would appreciate your taking a few minutes to respond to the following questions. We welcome your comments and read each form and letter we receive. When completed, please return to the following:

Fiction Editor
Heartsong Presents
PO Box 719
Uhrichsville, Ohio 44683

1. Did you enjoy reading *Broken Bow* by Irene Brand?
   ❑ Very much! I would like to see more books by this author!
   ❑ Moderately. I would have enjoyed it more if

   _____

   _____

   _____

2. Are you a member of **Heartsong Presents**?   ❑ Yes ❑ No
   If no, where did you purchase this book? _____

   _____

3. How would you rate, on a scale from 1 (poor) to 5 (superior), the cover design? _____

4. On a scale from 1 (poor) to 10 (superior), please rate the following elements.

   _____ Heroine   _____ Plot
   _____ Hero   _____ Inspirational theme
   _____ Setting   _____ Secondary characters

5. These characters were special because? _____

_____

_____

6. How has this book inspired your life? _____

_____

_____

7. What settings would you like to see covered in future
   Heartsong Presents books? _____

_____

_____

8. What are some inspirational themes you would like to see
   treated in future books? _____

_____

_____

9. Would you be interested in reading other **Heartsong
   Presents** titles? ❏ Yes   ❏ No

10. Please check your age range:
    ❏ Under 18   ❏ 18-24
    ❏ 25-34   ❏ 35-45
    ❏ 46-55   ❏ Over 55

Name _____

Occupation _____

Address _____

City, State, Zip _____

The
Spinster Brides
OF CACTUS CORNER

4 stories in 1

Unmarried women committed to helping orphaned children in their community aren't necessarily looking for love when romance sweeps into their small Arizona town.

Frances Devine, Lena Nelson Dooley, Vickie McDonough, and Jeri Odell share the stories of four spinster Arizonans who happen upon love in the midst of an orphanage ministry.

Historical, paperback, 352 pages, 5³⁄₁₆" x 8"

Please send me ____ copies of *The Spinster Brides of Cactus Corner*.
I am enclosing $6.97 for each.
(Please add $3.00 to cover postage and handling per order. OH add 7% tax.
If outside the U.S. please call 740-922-7280 for shipping charges.)

Name_____

Address _____

City, State, Zip _____

To place a credit card order, call 1-740-922-7280.
Send to: Heartsong Presents Readers' Service, PO Box 721, Uhrichsville, OH 44683